Spirit Trail

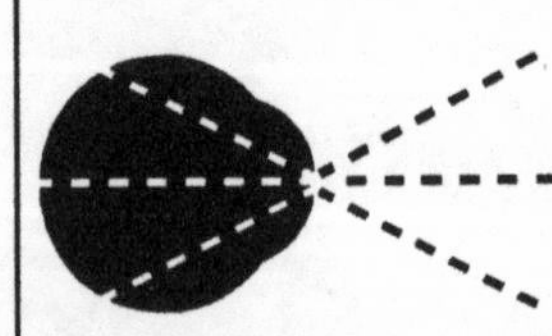

THE GHOSTRIDER SERIES

Spirit Trail

Darrel Sparkman

THORNDIKE PRESS
A part of Gale, a Cengage Company

Farmington Hills, Mich • San Francisco • New York • Waterville, Maine
Meriden, Conn • Mason, Ohio • Chicago

Thorndike Press, a part of Gale, a Cengage Company.

Thorndike Press® Large Print Western.
The text of this Large Print edition is unabridged.
Other aspects of the book may vary from the original edition.
Set in 16 pt. Plantin.

LIBRARY OF CONGRESS CIP DATA ON FILE.
CATALOGUING IN PUBLICATION FOR THIS BOOK
IS AVAILABLE FROM THE LIBRARY OF CONGRESS

ISBN-13: 978-1-4328-5304-4 (hardcover)

Published in 2018 by arrangement with Galway Press, an imprint of Oghma Creative Media

Printed in Mexico
1 2 3 4 5 6 7 22 21 20 19 18

AUTHOR'S NOTE

I never studied much, school wasn't a big interest for me. In retrospect, I wish I had. But, what I did was read. Didn't have much of a childhood, so I read to escape I suppose. Four to five books a week — from middle school into adulthood. You name it — I read it. Changing schools over twenty times from kindergarten to twelfth grade gave me insight into people and circumstances — and the value of standing your ground. I loved science fiction, but when the genre morphed to fantasy, I dropped out. Being raised in rural America bent me toward adventure novels and westerns, and I've been writing since I was young. Reading one adventure novel and wanting to get on to the next gave me the style in my writing of picking a week or so in the protagonist's life and riding hell-bent from problem to solution. My heroes are prone to suddenness of action and intent. Writing can exorcise your demons, give you the pleasure of a story well told, and drive you to distraction. But it is always a ride worth taking.

This book is dedicated to a man who told me to keep writing back in 1997, and that book turned into *Hallowed Ground.* Dusty Richards.

Thanks, Dusty. Live long and prosper.

. . . A noble race, but they are gone,
With their old forests wide and deep,
And we have built our homes upon
Fields where their generations
sleep. . . .

The Disinterred Warrior
The Poetical Works of
William Cullen Bryant 1878

One

Sean MacLeod stood on the front porch of his cabin, deep in the forest surrounding the upper Missouri River. He paused to lace up his leather boots, tucking the pant legs of his buckskins inside. His shirt was still inside the cabin, and the early May morning was cool on his skin. He took a deep breath, enjoying the curious and merging light of early morning when the sun was up but hadn't penetrated to the depths of the forest. It had rained the past two days, and the forest air smelled fresh and clean. The sleepy calls of the finches and sparrows came from the bushes behind the cabin. High above, in the bright morning sun, an eagle floated on the warming breeze.

The hard sound of a crow, calling in the distance, interrupted the peaceful sounds of the morning. He listened intently for a moment. No other calls answered the first, which was odd in itself since crows are usually gregarious creatures. He didn't like that . . . not at all.

He and his four brothers had cleared this land and built the cabin a year ago. Grass was finally starting to grow and they'd transplanted several blooming bushes like sumac and wild rose. Sean was proud of what they'd accomplished in a short amount of time and was content with his world. Now he had a new home, beautiful wife, and son.

Above the low, rushing sound of the river just over the ridge came the ringing of a hammer on metal. The blacksmith at the trading post was up and working.

Sean smiled. When the blacksmith, Finias MacGregor, was up and working . . . everybody was up because he made so much noise. The trading post of his adopted father would be open for business. Angus MacLeod had opened his trading post years before close to where the Yellowstone River came into the upper Missouri. Now, with pressure from competing fur companies, business was slow and Angus talked of selling out to one of the competitors and moving on. Sean's adopted status put him pretty far down the list of family hierarchy. With all the brothers above him there wouldn't be an inheritance, but that was all right. It would be better to make his own way and not depend on someone else.

At twenty years of age, and full-grown since he was fourteen, Sean was a veteran of many trips up and down the river and had crossed through the forests many times. It was always a dangerous journey, and he had the scars to prove it. He was certain he could provide for his family. It was a good thing Angie couldn't care less about riches. All she seemed to want was the baby and her husband. If the trading post closed or moved, he and Angie would stay in their home.

Just as strong arms encircled his waist and he felt a naked, soft body pressed against his back, the cry of young Angus sounded from inside the cabin.

Rapid-fire French came from behind him in a muttered curse and he laughed. "Such a dirty mouth."

She tightened her grip with her left hand while her right hand wandered lower. "You didn't mind my dirty mouth last night."

He turned inside her arms and brought her to him, pulling gently on the back of her long, black hair until she lifted her lips to his. "Angie, you know how I love you." He kissed her again, holding her tight until she fought for breath and sagged against him. "To the end of time." He pushed her away with a chuckle and a swat to her butt. "Now go feed the boy. And put some clothes on."

She jumped from the swat and pretended to pout. "I'd hoped we would have some time for ourselves this morning."

Sean shook his head, smiling ruefully. She was insatiable, and he loved her for it.

His gaze lingered on her body, causing him to doubt his words even as he uttered them. "Tonight." He didn't want to wait until nightfall.

She paused at the door and turned to look at him, her silhouette painted by the soft glow of the fireplace. It was obvious she was aroused. He marveled at her beauty. Her long, black hair hung to her waist and framed dark, brown eyes. Expressive eyes. Her skin had an alabaster glow, and when no one was around but the two of them, she loved to show it. Young Angus was a year old today, and her body had regained its shape. God, she was beautiful.

The raucous call of the crow came again, this time from another direction. Watching the forest closely, he backed up to the door. Just inside and within easy reach was his Kentucky rifle. It always stood beside the door, along with a musket. He charged both weapons with fresh powder every morning so they'd be ready and waiting. It was a morning ritual with little meaning since they were at peace with all the tribes, but he did it anyway. After a few minutes of watching and listening, he relaxed and went inside.

Angie had dressed in her blue homespun dress, with a low bodice bordered in lace. She'd put her long hair up in a bun, adorned with a perky little white lace hat. When he'd made fun of the hat, she'd told him angrily that all French women wore them. He was smart enough not to argue.

She had the top of her dress off her shoulders and pulled down as she fed little Angus, rocking serenely as she watched Sean come in the door. He stood watching her for a moment.

"That's a beautiful sight, Angie. I never tire of watching you. If I had a painting of you like this, I'd cherish it forever."

She smiled at him and said in a mocking tone, "You'd better just paint it in your memory. I don't think you'd want some itinerant painter to see me like this. You know, sometimes I wish you would tire of me a little. The way I feel, we may have another mouth to feed in a few months."

"I can't see myself ever tiring of you, and you damn well know it." His voice was gruff with emotion as he watched her.

Turning her attention back to the baby, she switched him to her other breast. "This boy eats as much as you do."

He bent to kiss her forehead, and then kissed his son on the head. "Yes, but men my size can't live on milk alone."

Angie shoved him away with a laugh, and then pointed toward the stove. "Go and build up your strength. There's meat in the fry pan, and there should be bread and milk left." She caressed the boy as he suckled. "Look at him. He's already big for his age, and turning blond. He'll be a big man like his father." She giggled and looked up at him.

He looked at her quizzically. "What?"

"I'm just thinking. You stick out like a sore thumb, you know. Everyone around here is short, with dark coloring. Most of the trappers, your family, and the Cree Indians are all that way. I would pass for a Cree maiden. But you are much taller and bigger." She looked at him slyly. "And easily the most handsome. Some of my friends are jealous and wonder if you'll take a second wife."

He shook his head and smiled at her. She always made him feel ten feet tall. "That'll never happen."

She gave him a languid look. "Oh, I don't

know. If you keep me having babies just so you can watch them suckle, I may need the help."

Eating breakfast, and listening to her sing softly to the feeding baby, he thought of the day he met her.

In the fall of the year 1818, business had gone well at the trading post. After the buying season was over, Sean and his brothers loaded most of the furs bought during the summer onto barges and sent them, along with armed guards, down the river to market. Some of the furs would go to Canada, and part would go south to Kawsmouth at the junction of the Kaw and Missouri rivers. The rest would go east to Saint Louis. There would be a time of rest and rebuilding during the winter months.

Sean watched a wide canoe drift up to their dock, paddled by two men. Their cargo was in the center covered by buffalo robes, and it was odd for them to be trading this late in the year. The furs would be very low quality. But, on closer inspection, the canoe rode too high in the water to be loaded down with furs. *Curious.*

As the men disembarked and tied up the canoe, Angus was suddenly by Sean's side, holding out a rifle. Taking it from his father, his eyes never left the men coming toward them. "Who are they?"

He'd never heard such venom from his father. "It's Baptiste Charbonneau and his partner in crime, Santee." A gasp came from within the store as his mother heard the words. "They deal in slaves, not furs. I can't believe they would dare to stop here. Be careful, Sean. Charbonneau has killed many men. He's a sneaky bastard."

Sean stepped out of the trading post's door to meet them, his rifle pointed at Charbonneau's belly. "What's your business here?"

The men skidded to a stop, eyeing the rifle pointed at them. Both were armed with muskets, but didn't attempt to use them. Each had a knife and pipe ax at their waists. The man called Santee wore greasy buckskins and a leather wide-brimmed hat. His buckskins looked so stiff with dirt he could take them off and stand them in a corner. He was a small man whose face showed the ravages of bad living and whiskey, with watery eyes and a blue-veined nose red as an apple. It was an education to watch him fidget in place, casting eyes toward the store. Sean prayed he'd never need a drink that bad.

Charbonneau was the direct opposite. A

huge man, standing well over six feet, he wore homespun pants and a loose red shirt. Leather boots came to his knees. He grinned at them as he stopped, putting on an expansive air of being everyone's best friend.

Looking past Sean toward Angus, he said. "Ah, my friend Angus MacLeod. Long time, no? We just stopped by to do a little trading. My friend Santee has been without a drink for a week." He pointed at his partner and laughed. "As you can see, he needs a shot of whiskey."

"He needs a shot, all right. But not of whiskey. More like a lead ball." Angus spoke contemptuously. "We don't need your kind here. You're not wanted. It will take us days to rid the post of the stink of your presence."

Charbonneau jumped forward, his face flushed with anger, only to stop when Sean buried the barrel of his rifle in the man's gut.

"Bad idea."

Charbonneau backed up, rubbing his belly and looking vehemently at Sean. "I don't know you."

"You don't want to," he said, emphasizing the answer by another jab in the gut with the rifle.

From behind the slavers, toward the river,

there was a muffled scream. It looked like something was struggling under the covered cargo on the canoe. Suddenly, a girl leaped from the canoe onto the dock, throwing aside the buffalo robe. When she saw the cluster of men, she ran toward them, keeping a wide berth around Santee and Charbonneau.

When she caught her breath, she started talking rapidly in French, and then when she saw Sean didn't understand, repeated it slower in English. "Please. My name is Angelina Delavault and I need your help."

Charbonneau moved swiftly and tried to grab her, but she shrank away from him. "Look here, you. . . ."

Sean grabbed his arm, spinning him away. "Ease up, mister. That's no way to treat a lady."

The Frenchman fought against his grip. "That's no lady, as you call her. She's just a servant, and a damned uppity one, too."

Sean looked at her. The torn white blouse barely covered her breasts and she wore a buckskin skirt that had seen better days on a much larger woman. Dirty and scuffed moccasins were on her feet. She was poorly dressed, but held her head high. Even under all the grime, she was beautiful. He could tell she'd been tied up by the red, chafed marks on her wrists.

"You'd be pretty if you had a bath," he said, mentally kicking himself as soon as the words came out.

Surprisingly, she didn't take offense. "I'd love to have a bath." She smiled and looked directly at him, and it seemed in that moment the world narrowed to just the two of them. "But that bastard Charbonneau wants to help me."

Looking back, he fell in love with her at that moment. Even with her troubles, she had spirit and a sense of humor.

Charbonneau again tried to take control. "Hey, I bought her indenture from some folks upriver a few days ago, and she'll do as I say."

Angus spoke up in a mocking voice. "Can you prove this? You have papers?"

Charbonneau smiled, deprecatingly as he shrugged. "Yeah, somewhere."

Sean turned back to the girl. "You're indentured?"

She shook her head, holding his gaze with her own. "Stolen."

"She's lying. It's her word against ours. She's just a flighty girl who doesn't know what she's saying. That's why the people got rid of her." Both the slavers eased back toward their canoe.

Sean started after them, but Angus stopped him. "We'll have no bloodshed this day." Then he shifted his attention to the slavers. "Charbonneau, look around you. There are at least fifty men in my employ. They all know you. I'll also send word to the other posts along the river. If you return to this area, my men will have permission to kill you. Don't ever come back."

Charbonneau stood on the little pier, looking at them. Even at the distance, it was easy to see the hatred in his eyes. "It's a free country and you can't keep —"

The ball from Sean's rifle threw up splinters between the man's feet. He immediately reached out and Angus handed him another rifle.

It took the two men about a minute to jump into their canoe and paddle down the river and out of sight.

"We should have killed them. We're going to regret this," Sean said, watching the men disappear.

Angus snorted. "That's your Welsh blood talking. Killing shouldn't come so easy. Besides, we have no actual proof."

"There are no courts here. I think we have proof enough and she's standing before us." He turned to the girl. "Were you alone in the canoe?" He was worried that they should have checked under those robes.

"It was just me." Now that the ordeal was over, she was shaking and trying not to cry.

He took Angelina by the hand, led her into the post, and explained the situation to his mother. Before Mary married Angus, her name was Sparrow. She was a Cree Indian, and even Angus would admit she ruled the trading post and all who stepped into it. She immediately took the girl toward the living quarters in the back, but not before giving her husband a dark, meaningful glance. Sean thought she agreed with him about killing the slavers.

When they talked to her, they found out Angelina's parents died in a raid. The raiders were a western tribe she'd never seen before she was captured. Soon after, Charbonneau bought her. Since all her family had died, she stayed with them at the post and became like a daughter to Mary.

She followed Sean around constantly — not that he minded — and they often talked for hours. A few months later, Mary suggested it was time he took a wife and that Angie was a prime candidate. Somehow, Angie agreed. He didn't resist either of them.

His thoughts were brought back to the present when Angie got up from her rocker, sat little Angus down on a rug to play, and came to their rough-hewn table.

She nudged him with her thigh as she stood beside him, rubbing his shoulders with her strong hands. "I mended your shirt and it's hanging by the door. Don't be late this evening. Remember, I'm going to fix a special supper for you and have a cake for little Angus. Maybe some bear meat or catamount will help build up your strength for later. You seem a little tired this morning."

"Don't worry about my strength, woman." He grabbed at her and she laughed, avoiding his grasp. He couldn't keep his hands off her, and she knew it. "What will you do today?"

"Little Fawn is coming over later and we'll work on her new dress. We should have it finished today." She smiled at him and giggled. "There is a boy she wants to show it to. Knowing her, I'm not sure how long it'll stay on her."

He nodded and laughed at her joke. He knew and approved of her friendship with the Cree women living close to the post, even if their ways were different. Angie had laughed at him once and informed him the ways of the French were a lot different from the English or Scots too, and that's why he loved her so much. He couldn't disagree.

He turned serious a moment. "Be careful going out today. There's a new camp over by the river, and I heard they're Bloods. They're new to us."

She shrugged it off. "Don't worry. We're at peace with the tribes, and the Cree are allied to the Blackfoot so these Kaini won't let them make trouble. Although, Little Fawn told me yesterday they won't do trade with the post, and are trying to discourage everyone else from trading with us."

"Well, they've probably been paid off by Hudson's Bay or American Fur to create a rift between us. They'll probably be gone soon, but be careful of them. Just fire a shot and barricade the door if anything looks wrong, and we'll come runnin'. We're only a couple of minutes away, over the ridge."

She kissed him on the cheek. "You worry too much. Now, go. I have work to do."

Sean walked into the front door of the trading post and stopped a moment to enjoy the sights and smells of all the goods for trade. Aside from the furs stacked to the ceiling at one end of the store, there were spices and dried herbs. Gunpowder and oil, metal tools and arrowheads, along with cloth and cooking utensils covered the walls and benches. Leather English-style saddles and bags were prominent in one corner with bridles and halters.

Even growing up, he'd always loved the store. His mother waved as she and a couple of helpers stacked furs in a corner. He turned and could see Angus overseeing the loading of a barge down by the dock. The blacksmith cursed and yelled as he tried to catch one of the horses that needed shoeing. Two men came out to help and they finally herded the horse, a piebald mare, into a chute built in a corner of the corral.

Horses were becoming good trade items, if they could keep thieves from stealing them. The horses weren't too common until recently. Since they'd finally arrived in the North Country, mainly from the Nez Perce and southern tribes, it seemed as if everyone wanted one. Whether it was for a pack animal, or to ride, horses saved a ton of work and time.

Walking into the store, he was immediately immersed in haggling and trading with a couple of trappers who said they'd just come in from the Yellowstone. He'd never seen them before, nor had anyone else. It was irritating because they didn't seem to have many furs, or have much interest in trading. He felt like they were just haggling to waste his time. By the time he finished with them, it was midmorning and he paused for a drink of cool water.

The long-handled dipper fell to the floor as his brother Daniel came bursting through the door, wide-eyed and yelling. "Sean, there's smoke coming from over the ridge. It looks like from your place."

He didn't waste time talking as he exploded out of the door and outdistanced everyone in the race to his home. He could hear several men running behind him, making little sound. He knew they were veteran fighters and Sean knew Angus would keep a good contingent back to guard the post in case this was an attack.

He stopped at the edge of the clearing, and for a moment it was as if he'd run into a wall and couldn't drag his feet forward. Fire was every settler's nightmare, and one reason many kept to their earthen floors, so sparks from the fireplace wouldn't catch hold. The roof of the cabin was already falling in from the flames shooting high into the sky. Smoke and sparks from burning embers floated lazily back to the ground. All hope of an accidental fire from their fireplace left his mind when he saw the bodies at the center of the clearing, next to an outside table and chopping block. He broke into a stumbling run. At the edge of his vision, he could see men from the post fanning out and surrounding the clearing.

He came to Little Fawn first, her body sprawled out and riddled with arrows. The new dress she was so proud of was torn and dirty at the foot of her naked body. He stopped for a moment, his heart in his throat, afraid to go forward. Finally, he steeled himself and went the final steps to Angie's body. She lay between two overturned, homemade chairs.

Kneeling beside her, his hands reached for her and then stopped. She, like Little Fawn, was naked and lay on her side facing away from him, her backside muddy from blood mingling with dirt. Both her legs pointed in impossible angles, and blood covered her from what seemed like hundreds of wounds. His eyes blurred with tears as he saw all the cuts and scratches on her. Like wild animals playing with their prey, they had taken their time with her. His heart nearly stopped when she groaned.

Gently rolling her over, he held her head in his lap. She'd fought them . . . fought them hard. Her fingernails were torn and a couple had bits of flesh hanging from them. There was a stab wound just under her ribs, a killing blow administered after they were through with her. The blood from the wound barely trickled. He shook his head. There was no hope. His tears dripped on her face as he watched her struggle a moment against the pain, and then she seemed to relax and looked up at him. It nearly killed him that she tried to smile, only to have it end in a grimace.

Her voice came out in a feathery soft whisper. "I'm sorry." She clutched at his arm, pulling at him. In a stronger voice, she said, "Angus?"

He looked at her with blurry eyes, shaking his head and he could tell she knew. "I love. . . ." He stopped. She was staring at him, but the light in her eyes was gone, never to shine again.

With a deep cry of anguish, he pulled her body to him. He didn't know how long he held her, until he noticed a ring of feet and legs surrounding him. At the touch of a hand on his shoulder, he looked up and his mother was there.

"Let us have her, Sean." Tears streaked down her cheeks. "Let us have her." Behind her were his brothers' wives, and they were all openly crying. Daniel's wife held a blanket.

They helped him to his feet as the women

covered his wife with the blanket and tried in vain to straighten her broken body. Finally, they helped the men put her on a plank to carry away. It wasn't until they moved her that he saw what her body was covering.

Stooping, he picked up a medicine bag usually worn around a warrior's neck, and a red sash of cloth torn off during the struggle. His fist closed around the medicine bag.

Looking in the distance with a fierce anger showing on his face that made men step away from him, he spoke the condemnation. "Kaini! The Blood clan of the Blackfoot."

One of the trappers who stayed around the post came to them holding a handful of arrows. "These are all Blackfoot arrows." The man spoke to Angus instead of Sean, handing him an arrow and pointing out the markings. "They didn't pick up their arrows, which is strange because they had time to do it." The man shook his head. "They always pick them up if they can. They don't like makin' arrows any better than we do."

"They must have been promised more." Angus broke the arrow in half, throwing the pieces into the dirt. "It looks like they got plenty of horses too."

His brother Daniel came walking up. He was the eldest of all the brothers and second only to Angus at the post. "I'm sorry, Sean. It'll be hours before the ashes are cool enough to find little Angus."

They all turned as one and looked at the still burning home. One of the men said in a hopeful voice, "Maybe they took the boy with them?"

"No." Sean could barely speak. "He's too young to take along, and there weren't any women in that camp to care for him. I just hope they killed him before he burned." His voice broke before he continued. "It's my fault. I should have known . . . should've been more careful."

Another party of about twenty men carrying long rifles loped into the clearing from the direction of the river. One of the men looked at Angus and shook his head. The men responsible for the killings were gone.

Daniel spoke to his father urgently, pulling at his sleeve. "If we leave now, we can catch those bastards. Let me take some men."

"No. Did you notice the Cree aren't going crazy at the death of Little Fawn? Something's going on and we can't leave the post undermanned. At least, not now. They may be trying to draw us out and leave it unprotected."

At his words, the men headed back toward the post. Some drug their feet in reluctance, some cast angry looks back at Angus MacLeod, but they all went.

He could hear his brother talking to his father, but the roaring in his ears nearly drowned him out. "What about Sean?"

"Just leave him, but post guards around the area." Angus watched his adopted son awhile. Mary was just coming back from the post and he stopped her from going to Sean, shaking his head. He pulled her to him and hugged her. "You know his history. Right now, there is a war going on inside him for his soul. I doubt if he knows we're here. We'll know in the morning if he is ours, or if he's returned to his ancestors." Together, holding hands, they turned and walked away.

Sean heard all this as he stood staring at the house that had become his son's funeral pyre, watching the flames destroy all his hopes and dreams. Images of Angie and little Angus filled his mind, but they were images of laughter and intimate moments.

Finally, he fell to his knees. He thought he should cry and try to mourn for his wife and son, but all he felt was deep anger. An inward heat burned at him with a fire greater than the one before him. A log popped in the inferno of their home and sent more flames into the air. As he watched, his mind filled with visions he'd never seen before, visions of fire and battle, of the clashing of metal and men fighting for their lives and screaming their anger. He violently shook his head and couldn't dislodge the visions, and when he closed his eyes, it was worse.

In the early hours of the next morning, Sean found the charred body of little Angus where he'd been left in his crib and wrapped him in his shirt, covered with his mother's blood, offering a silent prayer of guilt and apology. He should've been a better father. He should've protected them. Should have. The litany went on in his mind without pause or absolution.

When he heard people coming, he was already placing his son in a grave. Bare to the waist and covered in ashes, he locked gazes with his father a moment, and then watched as Angus turned abruptly and walked back toward the post.

A few more men showed up with shovels. "Is this where you want Angie's grave?" one of his brothers asked. When he nodded, they started digging.

The sun was high in the sky when they finished. All the words that needed to be said had been murmured in quiet deference. His mother stood close by, along with all his brothers and their wives. When he looked at the women, he expected to see sadness, but instead saw fear. He didn't blame them. It was supposed to be a time of peace. Most had heard of this kind of violence, but none had seen it in their young lives. They clung tightly to their husbands, seeking reassurance the men couldn't give.

Angus walked up to him leading a roan stallion already saddled. There was a bedroll on the back and food pouches hung from the back of the saddle. His rifle, longbow, and skinning knife hung across the front of the horse. All the arrows they'd found were put in a pouch and hung with his bow. He relished the responsibility of sending the arrows back to their owners.

Sean stared at his father with sadness. It looked as if the man had aged in the last few hours. "How did you know?"

Angus shrugged his massive shoulders. "You should see yourself. Your eyes are cold as ice. While you look calm, I sense anger and a thirst for blood that may never be slaked." Angus held his hand up, stopping

Sean's response. "No one blames you for how you feel. Would it do us any good to ask you to stay? We may need the help if they attack again."

"You have enough men to defend the post." He put his hand on his father's shoulder and squeezed. "I can't stay. And be assured that with every day that passes, the numbers of our enemies will be less."

"It's war, then?"

He was already looking toward the forest. "For me, not for you."

"I could ask for volunteers. We could send some men with you."

He shook his head. "The men have families and you need them here. Their interests are here and this is for me alone."

"It doesn't work that way, Sean. What they did to your family, they did to all of us. We may react in different ways, but we are still family. If you're at war, so are we." Angus looked around the clearing at his family and Cree friends that circled them and sighed. "Well, we'll hold out for a while. We have many friends."

"I'm sorry."

"Don't be. You didn't seek this trouble and must deal with it your own way. Besides, we only had a tenuous hold on you from the start, and I knew this day might come.

Things may have been different had your family lived. They were your anchor." He drew his hand over his face and sighed. "Say goodbye to your mother and brothers and be on your way. Don't drag it out and make the pain worse. Remember the good times."

Before Sean could turn to his family, a collective gasp came from one side of the crowd. The circle of people parted to show an old man leading a horse into the clearing. The horse was a Palouse stallion and anyone could see it was a trained warhorse of the Nez Perce. He noticed his own horse shying away from it in fear. The Blackfoot and Nez Perce were deadly enemies and there was no doubt where the horse had come from. It was the spoils of battle.

The old man came to stand a few feet in front of them. His once great frame had shrunk with age, but he held himself straight with pride. A single eagle feather adorned his scalp lock, and his buckskins looked soft and new.

"Bear Hunter." Angus breathed softly, taking a step toward the man. "We thought you were dead."

"Soon," the old man replied softly, and inclined his head toward Angus. "Soon enough, I will go away. But, the spirits give me no rest and have led me here to do one last thing."

Sean was irritated at the interruption. "Who is this man?"

Angus turned to him. "This is Bear Hunter, a great warrior. He's the one who brought you to us many years ago."

"I will speak!" The old man's voice carried the ring of authority. Few tribes had any sort of written language. Many of the chiefs and warriors were great orators and the spoken word passed their history down from generation to generation. The circle of Cree Indians and trappers from the post crept closer to hear what he had to say.

The man drew himself up and Sean could see the once proud warrior that he'd been. "I am Bear Hunter of the Piikani, the Piegan Blackfoot."

People in the crowd repeated his words to those too far away to hear.

"When you were a small child, our people fought a great battle at a place we called Crossed Timbers. It was a remembered battle and your mother and father killed many of our people. I watched in wonder as your wounded mother killed even more men as she stood over the body of her husband. Our young men were full of pride, and since she fought by the knife, they sought to kill her as she fought them . . . by the knife.

She was fierce and proud. We had never seen anyone such as them. The warrior woman finally fell from our arrows, and each of us walked by to touch their yellow hair and count coup. They were mighty warriors. In their honor, we buried them and did not defile their bodies. We heard later that they were from a land far away and once battle came to them, they went crazy with battle lust. This I have seen. It is true."

Bear Hunter took a step toward him and looked deep into his eyes a moment. He felt the old man was looking into his soul and shook his head to get away from the stare. "When they were finally killed, we saw they were protecting you. Even though you were a child, our braves saw the same fierceness in your eyes, and they wanted to kill you as we would a wolf cub, but I would not let them. I tied your hands and took you away."

Sean thought he saw a gleam of a smile in the old man's eyes.

"We had to gag you or you would have cut us with your teeth and I finally had to knock you in the head to stop you." Bear Hunter drew himself up to his full height and said, "I do not know of this land you came from. I can only thank the Great Spirit no more of you have come."

He turned to his horse, took a rolled

blanket down from it, and handed it to Sean. Curious, Sean knelt and unrolled the blanket out on the ground. The sun glittered off the blades.

"Fighting knives," Angus breathed out. "Spanish blades."

Bear Hunter nodded. "These are the knives your parents used in the battle after they sent all their arrows into our men. Our warriors finally had to swallow their pride and shoot them from afar. We could not get close without dying."

Sean stood, holding the two knives. Longer than a regular hunting knife and shorter than a saber or sword, the thin blades were bright in the noonday light. The handles were made of ivory or some kind of bone, and felt like an extension of his body.

Looking closely, he could see dried blood staining the blade close to the handle. The knives must not have been used or cleaned in all this time.

He looked at the old man. "If this is Blackfoot blood, it's fitting that I should return it."

Bear Hunter inclined his head, and then looked around at all the people and their anger. "All should know this. We are not at war with these people. Only the Kaini, or the Bloods, have taken the war trail. It is a bad thing they have done and I cannot see an end to it."

Turning back to Sean, he said, "I have known this day would come. Since I picked you up and held you close to my heart, I have known it. I could feel the spirit of your parents passed on to your heart. Now, the Spirit Trail has come to you. I feel sadness for you that it is a trail of vengeance and death. I am old and have seen too many winters. This thing I have learned in my time on this earth. Do not let this anger consume you, or it will eat your mind and your very living will be as death." He looked around the ring of faces. "This is all I have come to say. I will speak no more."

Bear Hunter strode forward and stripped Sean's stallion of its saddle and supplies. He then traded the horse Angus brought for Sean for the warhorse he'd ridden in on. With a spring in his step belying his age, the old Indian leaped on the back of his new horse. Holding his palm out toward the people gathered there, he wheeled the mount and yelled, "Kitatama'sino! I shall not return."

The Cree warriors responded in kind by raising their weapons above their heads and their voices in a mighty shout.

His father's voice caught his attention.

"Where will you go?"

He tore his eyes from the retreating warrior and looked at his father and mother. "Wherever they go, I'll follow." Realizing his words sounded like a marriage vow, he shrugged and turned to his new horse. "Honestly, I don't know."

"You will be tested. I've taught you all I know about trading, and living. And about fighting. Remember it. Most Indians know nothing about a rapier or sword. They only know the knife and tomahawk. Use your training well." Angus's deep voice seemed to catch in his throat a moment. "Don't flaunt your training, Sean. I only pray it will be enough."

He remembered the relentless training he and his brothers had received from Angus, usually during the slow winter months. Limber sticks and switches gave way to wooden swords, and then the real thing with padded clothing. Angus tried to temper the fighting with trading and books, but Sean had embraced the training early. The footwork during a fight and measuring an opponent's skill became almost like a dance. But it was a dance of death.

He looked at his father and gripped the man's shoulder with his hand. "You've treated me well and I thank you. Now, it's up to me to make my own way. If that journey is over dead Bloods, then so be it."

It was a beautiful horse, and it stood quietly as Sean put his saddle on it and tied on his gear. He scratched its ears and the animal finally acknowledged him by rolling its eyes and flicking its ears. Speaking softly, rubbing its neck and head, he waited until he was sure it was used to him.

"I'm going to name you Thunder and we will get our revenge against the Blackfoot."

After he mounted, he rode over to the graves of Angie and little Angus. The sun was warm on his shoulders, and the air was fresh and clean. The summer breeze blew the smoke to the north, away from the charred ruins of his home.

A sharp shake of his head pushed away the bad images and brought clarity to his mind. His family would never enjoy another day like this and he felt guilty that he could. Angie would never welcome the feel of the sun on her body again. With determination, he tossed away the sight of her mutilated body and kept the image in his mind of her nursing their son as the morning light caressed them through a window. He nearly reached out to touch her. *Angie.*

"You will be avenged."

Without another word, he turned toward the river to follow the trail of the Bloods.

TWO

Sean left the graves of his wife and son and rode to the camp of the Blackfoot, next to the Missouri River. The sun beat down on his shoulders and the heat was already stirring up the rotting smells of dead fish and offal on the riverbank. The camp was empty and showed signs of a hasty departure. Smoke still rose from a few campfires, and there was the bright splash of color in blankets left behind. A scruffy looking grey dog of questionable lineage nosed through a pile of bones and pieces of hide piled against a tree they had used for throwing a tomahawk for practice. Indians were usually cleaner than this, and would often dig holes to bury their trash and garbage.

Since it had rained a couple of days before, the easily seen trail of churned earth left by the retreating band of Indians skirted the river, heading downstream. He followed relentlessly. Thunder kept trying to pick up the pace, but he held him back to a steady and fast walk. It would be a long hunt, and the last thing he needed was a tired horse. Strangely, he felt no great sense of urgency. There was no doubt the Indians would eventually turn and fight. The timing of it really didn't matter to him. Soon or late, it was all the same.

Nearing dusk, he came to a small stream that fed into the larger Missouri River and found the trouble he was looking for. He'd already figured this would happen, just not this quickly. It was obvious their headlong rush to get away from the trading post was in fear of reprisal from the people settled there. They would have been outnumbered. But their pride wouldn't let them run long. They must have camped for the night and then waited to see who would show up in pursuit.

It was odd, the things that went through his mind. He'd been in dangerous situations before, but it seemed his senses were heightened to the point all of them screamed for attention. Although shaded by his hat, the sun was warm on his shoulders as he walked Thunder into the clearing. He could feel the horse trembling in anticipation, and reached a hand down to pat his sweaty shoulder. The sound of Thunder's hoof-falls measured a steady cadence, along with the sound of water rushing over a shallow riffle in the river. A camp robber blue jay fussed in the lower branches of a twisted pine next to the river. Buffeted by floods in the spring and fall, and nearly uprooted, the tree stubbornly clung to the earth.

He took a deep, calming breath of pungent river air filled with the smell of fresh water and an occasional dead fish or animal and the fragrance of pine and honeysuckle. He could find the river in the dark by smell alone. Drying his palms on his pant leg, his attention came to rest on the clearing before him.

A lone Indian stood in the clearing, his horse tied to a branch of a small tree, and he seemed to be waiting patiently. Beyond him and across the stream, several more braves on horseback were lined up to watch the action. This wasn't all of the band of Bloods, so the rest must have gone on. He carefully looked around. The last thing he needed was another warrior slipping in behind him.

As he'd heard from the Cree warriors, this act by the single warrior was the root and honor of the Blood clan. One, or many would stay behind to cover the retreat of the main body to ensure their safety. So be it.

The warrior waiting for him was a big, muscular man. He'd stripped to the waist, and his chest and arms were covered in grease, a favorite trick when wrestling an opponent. He'd seen it done many times in the wrestling bouts around the post. *No wrestling today, boy.* The Indian had a black palm print on each cheek, and red vermillion on his chest. The single eagle feather in his hair meant he'd joined the ranks of warriors by killing an enemy.

Sean glanced around again. Indians didn't care how an enemy died. An ambush would work as well as a frontal assault.

The Indian shifted his feet restlessly, his gaze and manner showing contempt for the white man, preening and showing off before his audience.

Sean decided to put on his own show and prove a point to the audience of Bloods.

Wrestling was popular among the tribes and this man looked overly muscled and confident, probably a champion in his village. Sean knew what he must do. This wouldn't be a wrestling match or any kind of test of strength. The warrior had a ceremonial pipe ax in his right hand, his left was empty, and he spread his arms wide in invitation.

Sean swung a leg over Thunder's neck and dropped lightly to the ground. The horse stopped immediately. Walking purposefully toward the man, he pulled his new fighting knife, knowing the sound of the blade leaving its metal sheath would be as loud as the cocking of a rifle, and never stopped advancing. The Indian's gaze dropped momentarily to the blade.

His adversary was right-handed, so he kept his knife in his right hand, a simple matter of logistics for what must be done. The bone handle was firm and felt molded to his palm. Instinctively, he knew it wouldn't slip.

When Sean was a couple of paces away, the Indian realized there would be no talk or boasting, and no pleading for mercy. With a startled expression, he pulled his arm back to strike with the ax and Sean simply ducked under his arm and silently walked a few more paces forward. In one simple move, the Indian was sliced open just under his rib cage. The warrior dropped to his knees with an anguished cry and his ax dropped from nerveless fingers.

The fight was short, brutal, and had the desired effect on the warriors across the stream. Sean stood facing them, outwardly calm, his knife dripping blood as it pointed at the ground. For a moment they were silent, spooked by something that wasn't supposed to happen and with a brutality that surprised them. It wasn't even a fight. It was a killing.

They fired at him with their muskets and bows, yelling and screaming their anger. The range was pretty far, and he watched them silently. He flinched as a piece of metal creased his arm, but didn't bother to look at the wound. One of the men started into the stream, digging his heels into the flanks of his horse, but a sharp command halted his advance. Behind him, he heard a strangled sigh. Glancing over his shoulder, he saw the warrior had bled out and died.

A shout from across the stream drew his attention. A different warrior was crossing the stream, his horse splashing through the shallow water, and the late afternoon sunlight glittered on the water flying from the horse's hooves. The man drew his bow as his horse pounded toward him, guiding the animal with his knees.

Just as the warrior released his arrow, Sean took a quick step to the left. The shot went wide, and Sean retreated to his horse and grabbed his Kentucky long rifle. When he turned, the Indian was almost on him and he shot him. The heavy fifty-caliber ball hit him in the chest and somersaulted him off the back of his horse. The Indian hit the ground in a loose heap and didn't move. His mount went on by and disappeared into the trees.

Loading his rifle, Sean watched the rest of the Indians. If they all charged now, he was dead. But they sat their horses and watched him, arguing with each other. Finally, one man crossed the stream and rode slowly toward him. His weapons were hanging from his horse and his arms were outspread, palms to the sky. Sean turned, gathered the reins and mounted Thunder.

When the warrior was close, he stopped and looked at the two fallen warriors, then raised his gaze to Sean's eyes. "I would take these warriors home. They died well."

Sean was having none of it. "They died as children, thinking because I'm white I'd be an easy kill." He watched the Indian closely, trying to provoke an attack.

"But they still fought." The Indian inclined his head slightly, anger burning in his eyes. "You are alone. Why do you follow us?"

Sean looked at him, not believing what he'd just heard. "You burn my home, kill my wife and son, and you wonder why I follow you? What manner of men are you? You are cowards and a stink upon this land. The mighty Kaini kill women and children when no men are present. I spit in your mothers' milk."

The warrior stiffened at the insult, his hand creeping toward his musket. "You are a MacLeod. You have no right to be here. White men have no place on this land."

Sean's rifle rose and pointed at the man's belly. If he killed this man, the rest would cross the water and attack, but it didn't matter to him one damned bit. "You came in peace, and I will honor that. If you wish, we can finish this between us. It's your choice."

The man's hands came back to rest in front of him. Ignoring Sean, he looked at the first warrior Sean killed. "Your medicine is great today, and you think you are ready to die. Another day, maybe your medicine is not so great and you will beg for death as you hang over a fire. You should sing your death song, for it is near. This man has brothers. They will come for you."

Sean hung his long rifle over the saddle horn and spread his hands wide from his body. His voice sounded like someone else to his own ears, someone cold and lifeless. "Perhaps I should let these brothers go free and only kill their women and babies. Would that make me brave like the mighty Bloods of the Blackfoot? This is how you wage war. I will not do this. Bring your cowards to me. I am alone. I'm sure it's the Blackfoot way to send twenty or thirty men to kill one lone white man. After all, that's how many of you it took to kill my wife and son."

"You're not afraid to die?" The warrior looked at him curiously and didn't seem to pay attention to his insults. "All men say this, but few men are ready."

He shrugged. "I'm a ghost already. It's just a matter of time before I go to join my family. But hear this. When I die, I'll be surrounded by the bodies of slain warriors."

They stared at each other a few moments, the white-hot hatred showing in the eyes of the warrior trying to break down the icy calm of the white man. Finally, the warrior spoke sharply over his shoulder and two of his men crossed the stream. They gathered the two empty horses and slung the dead men across their backs. Without a backward glance, they rode away.

"Why?" Sean's voice finally broke and was hoarse with emotion. "Why kill my family? They were not a threat to you."

The man shouted his answer so loud he spooked his own horse. "Whites do not belong here. This is our land. Piegan, Kaini, and Siksika all live here. No whites."

Sean's answer was bitter as he shook his head. "A lie is supposed to be the worst thing you can do in your clan. You don't even have a word for it. But you are living a lie. You sit on a horse brought into this country by the Spanish years ago. You traded your stinking robes, made out of animal skins, for blankets brought by the white men. You steal and trade muskets and rifles from white men. The copper pots and iron pans your women cook with were brought to you by white traders, along with nseedles to sew your buckskins so your ass doesn't freeze in the cold. Your very actions give the lie to your words. And Blackfoot land? This wasn't your land until you killed those who lived here before your people came. You kill because it's all you know and all you want to know."

The Indian was shaking his head. "This is not so. All want war. The only honor is in war. Even your whites from a different tribe make war against you. The French and English want you gone."

"And is this your honor, to kill defenseless women and children? Then you ran away! Do you brag of this? Sing songs of this, telling of your bravery?"

He saw a shift in the Indian's eyes. Maybe that got through.

"We were given much to make war. There can be no peace around you. Not now."

Sean looked closely at the man. "You were paid? Who paid you? Damn you. Who?"

With a contemptuous look over his shoulder, the warrior turned his horse and rode away to join his band.

As Sean watched the brave, he never wanted to shoot someone in the back as much as he did right then. And he really couldn't figure out why he was still alive. The warrior he'd been talking to took up a bow and sent an arrow into the tree next to him. From the instant it was launched, he could tell it wasn't at him, so he didn't react.

He guided Thunder over to the tree and took down the arrow. It had a piece of red cloth tied to it. Symbolic of what? The Blood Clan? Tired of games, he broke the arrow, spit on it, and threw it toward the watching Blackfoot. For a moment, they watched him and then at an abrupt command, turned and rode away.

He stood for a long time, the adrenaline draining from his body and leaving him weak. If the Bloods turned around and attacked, he wasn't sure he could lift a finger in his defense. He didn't remember if he got off his horse, or fell off, but he was suddenly bone tired and felt he didn't have the strength to move. He'd envisioned a pitched battle between him and the Bloods, in which he was prepared to die, and expected to. One thing he learned. Never think you know what other people are going to do.

He'd made the decision to follow them the instant he found Angie. It would be foolish and deadly to attack their camp. But lone stragglers would be fair game. He'd take a page out of their own book of war. They have to hunt sometime, and he would be waiting.

Gathering the reins of his horse, he strode into the forest. Finding a spot protected from the wind, he made camp. After taking off the saddle and bundles of supplies, and scratching the horse behind the ears for a moment, he staked Thunder out next to a patch of grass, and ate a piece of jerky from his pack. Taking a swig from his canteen, he drew a blanket around him and tried to sleep.

He tossed and turned while demons and spirits danced through his dreams. In one, he held Angie and his son, laughing at each other as they swam in a stream and in the next, he was crying to the heavens, holding her dead body in his arms. Warriors from a strange land, and the like he'd never seen, danced and screamed into the night. They had long blond hair and blue paint on their faces, their fighting knives flashing in the light. They screamed at him to awaken and join them, and they screamed revenge.

He came awake standing next to the tree that had been his backrest during the night, crouching and holding his knife, expecting an attack. No sound came to him except for his horse cropping grass a few feet away and his own hoarse panting. Wiping sweat from his eyes and controlling his ragged breathing, he finally realized it was only a dream and sheathed his weapon.

With a sigh, he settled with his back to the huge oak tree. It was his second day without Angie, and he could still smell her fragrance, taste her lips, and feel her body against him. He shuddered and wiped moisture from his eyes.

For a fleeting moment, he wished he'd died with them. It surely couldn't have been worse than this. *Soon enough. Soon enough.*

The next morning he woke before dawn and followed the Blood's trail at first light. Within a mile the path and churned earth of their war ponies broke apart in several directions. He thought this was a ruse to throw him, or anyone following, off their trail. Picking one trace, he followed it for several miles. The track switched back several times, but he was able to stay with it.

Every morning he woke with anger and determination. Every night he tried to sleep with visions of battle running through his mind. He was exhausted and the Bloods knew they were followed. Once an arrow flew from the woods and nicked his shoulder. He didn't know the Blackfoot word for coward but yelled it in English and then in Cree. Another time Thunder snorted and sidestepped something. They'd made a small pit and covered it with a blanket and sticks. The hole would have broken a horse's leg. The only sound from the forest was the wind in the trees.

He kept with this trail for several days until he finally lost it along the rocky shore of a small lake. Since the track went generally east, he kept that direction until late one evening, he came out on a bluff and saw an encampment below. Several tepees sat along a stream while a small horse herd grazed in the meadow on the other side. After watching the bustling activity around camp fires and tents, he decided to wait until morning. He backed away from the edge of the bluff and found a spot under the branches of a low hanging cedar. Hobbling Thunder on a patch of grass next to the tree, he rolled in his blanket and tried to sleep between the dreams.

Morning was a hint of rose in the east when he went to Thunder and began to put his pack and saddle on the horse. Chewing a piece of pemmican, he caught movement to his right. His hand swept down to the knife at his side and he felt a blow to his shoulder.

A small boy stood staring at him with eyes wide in determination and his mouth set in a grim line. He held a bow and carried small arrows, suitable for birds and rabbits, in a sheath at his side. *They teach them young.* He reached up and pulled the arrow from his shoulder. It had barely penetrated, but the tip was covered in blood. His emotions were conflicted. He should hate the boy but couldn't do it. "You are brave and have counted coup on me this day." The boy stood mute. He sighed and snapped the arrow into pieces, and then tossed them toward the young man's feet. "Are you Kaini?" The Indian nodded once.

"Tell them the Ghostrider is coming."

He gave the boy a half-hour start and then followed. The meadow, across the stream from the camp, was shrouded in a cool fog that came up to Thunder's belly. The camp had been dismantled and packed on horses and travois. The people seemed to be waiting for something and the answer to that came riding across the meadow toward him.

The man appeared to be an older, seasoned warrior and his horse's mane carried the hair of his conquests.

The Indian spoke gruffly. "It is said you are a ghost and cannot be killed." When Sean didn't reply, he raised his tomahawk. "I do not believe in ghosts."

The Blood charged and Thunder surprised them all by charging directly into the Indian's war pony. His superior size knocked the other horse down and his rider to the ground. The fight was short and brutal, lasting only a few moments.

He stood in the swirling mist and heard a collective moan from the Indians across the stream. They immediately began to file into the trees. Except for one.

The young boy looked small on the pony he rode. He stopped in front of Sean. "I have come for my father."

Sean turned and gathered the slain warrior's pony and hoisted the body up and across the blanket. The boy dismounted to help him tie the hands and feet under the pony's belly to keep the body from sliding off. When they were through, the boy mounted his horse and sat staring at him.

"I must go, my mother waits."

He looked past the boy and saw a lone woman sitting on a horse, her pack animals strung out behind her.

The boy spoke again. "If I turn my back, will you kill me? We are told not to trust the white man."

"Have I dishonored you today? Your father was a warrior and we fought as men. The Great Spirit decided who lives and who died. Be proud of him. Go and take care of your mother. She will need you."

"I will be a warrior one day. Maybe the Ghost will be around?"

He sighed, dismissing the challenge. "Tell your elders the Ghostrider has spoken. You are a warrior this day." He rubbed his shoulder, but the cut the boy's father had put on his chest hurt far worse. "Tell them you have blooded the Ghostrider and I have let you live."

The young warrior rode away, sitting straight and tall on his horse and taking his slain father home.

He watched the young man approach his mother. They sat a moment and then followed the rest of their clan into the trees.

What am I doing?

Thunder waited patiently while he came to a decision. The memory of Angie and little Angus was still fresh. But he knew what had to be done. The senseless killing had to stop. He turned his horse back the way he'd come.

He shook his head and scanned the trees. But would *they* let it stop?

In early October the first snow came. It began during the morning, starting with a light wind, and the soft hissing of the snowfall deadened all sound in the forest. By afternoon, it was a full-blown storm and Sean barely managed to make camp near a windbreak of close-growing aspen and cedar. Over three feet of snow covered the ground and some of the drifts in the open spaces were chest high on his horse. He was tired and so was Thunder.

In the last few months he was challenged twice. Each encounter took a little more out of him. The Bloods mentioned he was a ghost — that he couldn't be killed. What they didn't know was the schooling and training he and his brothers were given by Angus. Still, when he allowed himself to think, he knew it was time to leave. But where? This was all he knew.

When the horse was picketed in a small open space, he took a branch and cleared snow down to the cured brown grass below.

Satisfied the animal would at least have enough food to survive, he gathered a small amount of firewood for the morning. He chewed a ration of jerky and pemmican. Gazing at the surrounding hills growing dim with the fading light and heavy snow, he thought this gave a new meaning to a cold camp. Rolling himself into his heavy buffalo robe, he immediately fell into a deep sleep.

Sleeping under the buffalo robe, and completely covered with the night's snowfall, the insulating warmth of the snow kept him in an exhausted sleep. He nearly panicked when he heard Thunder stomping and snorting in warning. Indians of all tribes were masters of ambush and they hated the surprise of ambush more than anything. The mounds of snow around the campsite must have all looked alike to anyone searching for him. When Sean threw aside the robe and burst from under that snow-covered blanket almost under the Indian's feet, the startled brave gave a strangled bleat and hesitated a moment before he dropped his bow and made a slashing attack with his knife.

The hesitation cost the Indian his life, and Sean contemplated the body as he rubbed cold snow across a shallow cut on his ribs. It was close, but the Indian's hesitation allowed time for Sean to bring his own knife into play. Like most fights, it was over in a few frenzied seconds of physical action and desperation. On the river, he'd heard tall tales of combatants fighting for hours until both were so fatigued they couldn't go on. He'd have to see that to believe it.

Sean stood naked to the waist and panting, shivering as steam rose from his sweating body. He looked at the crumpled form in front of him and wondered just how long Lady Luck would continue to be on his side.

Shivering again, he reached under his heavy buffalo robe and pulled out a buckskin shirt. Putting it on, along with a heavy coat, he scanned the area while he brought his breathing under control. If it hadn't been for the extra foot of snow and a trained warhorse, he might not be alive. He was amazed the Indian hadn't just tried to steal the horse. Surely that would have been a greater prize than his scalp.

After checking for tracks in the new fallen snow and satisfied this was yet another lone Blackfoot brave out to count coup and kill the hated Ghostrider, he started a small fire with tinder and flint from his pouch, glad he'd had the sense to bring in some wood the night before and cover it with a piece of oilskin.

He walked over and took the hobble from Thunder's foreleg and rolled up the picket line. As the warhorse followed him back to the campfire, he chided himself for hobbling the horse at night. In the time they'd been together, Thunder hadn't shown any inclination to wander away from his camp. Scrounging around in his pack, he found some dried apples and fed one to the horse.

Rubbing Thunder's ears, he murmured to him. "Thanks for the warning, boy. I let myself get too tired and warm last night."

Sitting in front of his fire, warming his hands and flipping over the slice of venison in the iron skillet, he'd been hearing someone coming toward his camp for a couple of minutes. He was startled at first and nearly jumped for cover but figured the noise was intentional, just to let him know they were out there. No Indian would make that much noise. While he heard the noise coming from in front of him, Sean noticed Thunder faced a different way and his ears were fully forward at attention. And he hadn't heard any noise from that direction.

Two, then. And one of them is coming real careful.

The noise in front of him stopped. "Hello the camp." The man's voice was not loud, merely conversational.

"Come on in if you're friendly." Just in case, his rifle was close to hand and his coat unbuttoned for access to his fighting knife. He knew these were probably trappers, but it wouldn't hurt to be cautious.

"What if I'm not?"

Sean chuckled. "Then I'll make you drink my coffee."

A man stepped out of the brush, leading a horse and pack animal. Dressed for winter, he wore a fur robe and cap that obscured most of his face. His rifle was in a decorated sheath, but the man's hand was on the action so that didn't mean a lot. He'd seen people shoot right through the leather sheath. After looking around, and then watching Sean a moment, the man relaxed and walked up to the small fire.

"Name's Johnson," he said. "I smelled your fire, so I came to visit."

Sean set the skillet off and threw a couple more sticks on the fire. He set a pot of fresh snow over the flames to melt for coffee. "Tell your friend to come on in. It'll be warmer next to the fire."

Johnson looked at him a moment, then smiled. "You're no pilgrim." He whistled softly.

Off to his right, another figure rose from the brush and came in leading a horse. The person dropped the horse's reins next to Thunder and stopped to rub the warhorse behind the ears. His guess was confirmed when she moved the hood off her head and shook out her long, black hair. She carried a short musket and a long rifle hung on her horse by a leather strap. The woman paused, looking at the body sprawled a short distance away. Abruptly, she walked the few steps required, muttering something, and kicked the cooling body. It must have felt good to her, because she delivered another solid kick.

The trapper snorted. "Sorry about that. She don't like Blackfoot much, especially Bloods."

Sean just nodded, wondering at the real purpose of the visit. "Seems odd."

"What's odd?" The man brushed snow off a log so he could sit.

"Most trappers I meet up with are men traveling together for protection. I just meant it's odd to see a woman with you."

The man laughed softly. "The only odd thing would be if I traveled with a bunch of ugly men when this beautiful woman is available." He nodded to Sean. "Now, that would be odd."

Sean grinned at him. "Yeah, I can see your point."

He noticed their pack horses had a couple pair of snowshoes strapped to the packs. "Say, you wouldn't want to sell a pair of those snowshoes would you?"

"Naw . . . but they're pretty easy to make. Way things are lookin', we need to find a way to put them on the horses. The drifts are getting deep."

The woman came back, glancing with a smile at her man. She pulled a knife from her boot to cut a couple more slices of venison from the deer hanging from the tree, and then came to the fire. Taking the skillet, she placed it back on the fire and put in the meat. Tending to the fire, she settled back and ignored them.

Looking closely at her, Sean thought she looked familiar. "Do I know you folks? Seems like I've seen you before."

"Well." The trapper smiled and pulled his robe closer around him against the cold wind. It was hard to tell if a light snow was starting again, or if the wind was just blowing it around. Regardless, their clothes were getting a rime of white on the windward side. "Maybe you've seen her, but not me. Like I said, my name is Benjamin Johnson. This lady is a Cree Indian called Small Dove. And just so there's no misunderstandin', she's my wife. One of the Jesuit friars married us. I wouldn't want you to make any kind of mistake about that. Come to think of it, she might look familiar to you because she's Little Fawn's sister."

At Sean's look of surprise, Ben continued. "We were there when you lost your family. Not close enough to help, mind you. But close. It was a terrible thing."

Sean shook his head. "And Small Dove lost her sister. That kind of got lost in the shuffle, didn't it? I was so wound up over my loss, I didn't think. I'm sorry, Small Dove. Little Fawn was a good woman and a good friend to my wife. She didn't deserve what she got." Sean's memory hadn't faded since that day, and none of them deserved any of it.

He was curious, now. "So, what are you doing here? Wouldn't it be safer to stay around the post in the winter?"

The man and woman exchanged glances, and then she said softly, in English, "Tell him."

"I'm gettin' to it." He sounded irritated, but looked fondly at her. "Don't ever let a woman get under your skin, boy. She'll rule you night and day. Especially nights." He cut an embarrassed look at Sean. "Sorry, I guess you know all that."

At Sean's nod of assent, he continued.

"Look, a couple of weeks ago, the trading post closed up shop. After a couple of raids from the Blackfoot, the Cree left the area for parts unknown. I think part of them went north to Canada and the rest went south. It'll be hard on them to leave during the winter, but they thought it too dangerous to stay. Without their protection and help, the post suffered some losses. Trappers couldn't get to them without losing their hair, and the river folk couldn't get to them to trade. It was just too risky. Even some keelboats and barges got burned. You know how this part of the Missouri River is. The shallow parts can freeze up and if you get caught the Indians can walk right up to the boat.

"Anyway, old Angus said to hell with it. It only took a couple of days and they all headed west to Oregon territory, lock, stock and barrel. Seems like he had it all planned out, and had his wagons and oxen close by. I don't think he wanted to go, but once his Mary decided it was time, he had it figured right down to the last pony."

Sean felt a sense of loss. He hadn't really planned on going back, but the post had been a mental anchor to him. It was a safe haven. Now nothing like that would exist for him anymore. With his family gone, the sense of loneliness was a physical blow.

Trying to cover his emotions, he shrugged. "So, what are you doing here? Wouldn't it have been safer to go north into Canada?"

"Well, I don't much care for the Frenchies up north and besides, Angus gave all the trappers a message, just in case we run across you. Small Dove saw your tracks yesterday —"

"How'd she know they were mine?"

Johnson looked peeved at the interruption. "That Palouse has got to be the biggest horse in the country, and the tracks in the snow look like a herd of them African elephants went through. That's how. Anyway, she saw them tracks and then noticed someone was following you. I don't know what it is about these Cree Indians, but she can track a mouse across a flat rock. If I ever get lost out here, all I have to do is sit still and she'll come riding up. But like I said, she put two and two together and thought it might be you. We followed along just in case."

Sean looked at her. "It would have been nice to know that brave was out there last night."

Johnson looked embarrassed, digging around in the snow with the point of his knife. "With the snow and all, we kind of slept in this morning. The plan was to get here before daybreak and help or at least scare him off." Small Dove cast a wicked smile at him.

"The plan was to kill him before he got to you. Blackfoot don't scare worth a damn." Small Dove finally joined the conversation and Sean was surprised at her command of English. "Ben got distracted. We were on the way and back on that hill" — she pointed behind her — "when you were attacked." She met his gaze for a moment, and then giggled softly. "That warrior was probably half dead from fright when you rose up out of the snow. Funniest thing I ever saw. It startled me, and we were a ways off." She gave him a level stare. "You're a very good fighter. We shouldn't have worried."

A shadow passed from overhead and Sean glanced up to see the first vulture circling. It never took long, and wolves and coyotes wouldn't be far behind the carrion birds. All that would be a signpost and bring unwanted attention from watchful eyes.

"We should leave, soon."

Small Dove and Johnson attacked the venison with their small knives. Sean wasn't especially hungry after the killing, but ate a small portion. When he didn't finish, Small

Dove grabbed his remaining piece of meat and finished it off.

After they were done eating, she noticed the patch of red on his shirt. "The Blood marked you?"

Sean shrugged. "He damned near did more than that."

Small Dove went to her pack and brought back a small buckskin bag. She tossed part of its contents in the water he had boiling for coffee.

Dropping a white cloth in with it, she gestured at him. "Unbutton your coat and roll up the side of your shirt." Taking the cloth, she cleaned the cut.

When she applied the wet cloth to the cut, he nearly peed his pants. "What the hell is in that?"

Sean's breath came out in a hissing moan, and Johnson's expression screwed up in sympathy. "That's just gotta hurt."

The woman ignored both of them as she finished cleaning the wound. She raised his shirt further and looked at all his scars, not bashful at handling Sean's body. "You're starting to look like a damned Blood yourself."

Sean was always amazed how quickly the tribes picked up the art of cursing in English.

Finally, she dropped his shirt and gestured at the dead Indian. "Is this all you do with your life?"

"Stop it," Johnson interjected. "You got no right to say that, Small Dove."

She ignored her husband and looked up at Sean, who towered over her, and then shook her head. "You're just waiting to die. Someday there will be two men, or three, or maybe four. What will you do then? You will die." Her voice turned soft. "How many spirits of the Bloods will you take until it is enough? When will it end? Your wife was a good friend to our people . . . and to my sister. But she was a practical woman. She wouldn't want you to die. Not like this."

Sean looked at both of them. When he started to speak, she interrupted him by slapping him on the chest. "Go somewhere. Do something. Find a woman you can torment, as this man does me. Find life! Life is good." She glanced over her shoulder at her husband. "Sometimes."

Johnson chuckled a moment. "Woman sure speaks her mind, don't she? Trouble is she ain't often wrong." He wiped his hands on the front of his coat, and sheathed his knife. "Angus said to tell you, you can follow them to Oregon Territory if you want. You'll be welcome. If not, he said to go to

Kawsmouth at the bend in the Missouri River. He said you'd been to the post there and that they're holding a passel of furs and whatnot. It's yours to sell. He said that'd get you a start somewhere. It's all he could do for you."

Later, after they'd cleaned the campsite, Sean turned to them. "Thanks for the word from my folks. I appreciate it. Small Dove, thanks for your words. They were medicine arrows to my heart. I will count you as my friends, and I don't have many. Maybe I'll see you on the trail through the Yellowstone. If not, I'll leave word to where I am. I think we've all worn out our welcome around here. I'll be heading south. You both come and see me."

"Maybe we will," Johnson said. "Hear this. When you started this, it was just the Bloods. Now all three tribes of the Blackfoot are up in arms. Someone killed Bear Hunter shortly after you saw him, and they shot him in the back. It's a bad time to be around here, so we're gettin' the hell out. We'd travel with you, but I got the woman to think about. You're a damned Blackfoot magnet, and much as you may want to quit, they may not let you. As for us, we're just going to disappear."

They shook hands, and Small Dove

hugged him to her, an awkward movement with all the furs and robes they wore. In a moment, they were gone and he was alone again. He thought it strange how a simple hug from a woman can leave a man lonely and wanting more. Snow was falling again, and he was cold. And alone. He took a deep, cleansing breath, and the frigid air froze in his nostrils.

He walked over and looked at the dead Indian. He turned the stiffening body to his back. Although his face was slack in death and the eyes were dull and lifeless, he was still a good-looking boy. *Just a boy.* Would the killing of the hated Ghostrider have made him a warrior of great enough standing to allow him to miss the Sundance ceremony in the spring? Had Sean killed some relative? Maybe a brother? It was unknown. He shrugged and found he didn't really care. Like Bear Hunter had warned him, maybe he was losing his soul. Already gone.

It was an easy decision to make. With a deep sigh, he mounted Thunder and rode east to pick up the upper Missouri River. Like most travelers, he'd have to follow the river, especially in the winter. It would make the journey longer, but safer. He would travel south to the great bend in the river where the Kansas joined the Missouri. He knew Francois Chouteau had a post there, and that was where he'd find his furs. From that point, he didn't know. He'd miss his family and wished them well, but felt drawn to the south. Maybe he'd get away from the killing feud with the Bloods and find that woman Small Dove spoke of. Besides, he was tired of the winters in the North Country.

Three

Even with a milder than normal winter and the long gait of Sean's horse, it took them six months to make it to Kawsmouth. Following the river let him catch rides on barges and keelboats, but the upper Missouri is mostly shallow and given to freezing over. He spent a lot of time helping break ice when it was thin enough. When forced to travel by land, they both tired easily. Despite the mild winter, snowdrifts were four feet high on the passable trails. Thunder was a big horse, but deep snow can wear anything out, even a Palouse.

When he rode up to the north bank of the Missouri, across from Chouteau's post, it was early April. Sheets of rain pounded down through the trees, and he could barely see the surface of the water as showers marched across the river in erratic formation. A short pier jutted out into the river, but he stopped well short of approaching it.

He could only marvel at the bedlam in front of him, thinking of how the best description of confusion came from an old Indian when he said a man was ambushed and the man leaped on his horse and rode away in all directions.

At least a quarter mile of mud lay between him and the pier and the barge waiting there. The mud was hock deep on the horses and there were a couple off to the side, standing three-legged and abandoned. He wouldn't risk a broken leg on Thunder to enter the melee.

He counted at least thirty men fighting through the mud, pulling horses or carts, and cussing in more languages than he had ever heard. Looking across the river, the situation wasn't any better at the post. He turned his horse away. Behind him was a man leading three pack animals piled high with furs. With the rain and lightning, he hadn't heard him come up.

The man took off his wide-brimmed, floppy hat and gazed at the sky. "This rain is like a cow critter pissin' on a flat rock." As Sean chuckled at the apt description of a hard rain, the trapper jutted his chin toward the crowd below them. "Ya ever see the like?"

Sean looked back at the mess. "It looks

like everybody wants to get across the river at once. They must be giving away free liquor." He extended his hand. "My name's Sean MacLeod. Me and the horse just snuck out of Blackfoot country."

Shaking his hand, the man said, "I'm Jim Walker and you look like you just snuck out of somewhere. Your Palouse is about used up. How many Nez Perce did you have to plant to get that horse?"

Sean shook his head. "Not a one. An old Piegan medicine man traded me for it." He paused for effect. "Of course, I didn't ask him how he got the horse. Where'd you winter?" He only glanced at Walker, as both watched the muddy spectacle below them.

"I'll just bet that Piegan planted a few. Those horses are hard to come by, and there's no love lost between them and the Nez Perce." The trapper clamped his hat back on his head. "I came in from the Yellowstone country, and I'm lucky I got out with my hair. All three Blackfoot tribes are ranging far and wide. I heard the Cree went to Canada, and the Nez Perce went west into the Rockies. Nobody wants any part of those bloody Blackfoot. Dunno what got 'em so riled up." The man looked at him with a sly smile. "Of course, some folks make a livin' killin' Blackfoot."

Sean just shook his head, looking more closely at the man. "Only the Bloods. And now only when they bring it to me. I take it you know me."

"I've been to MacLeod's post a few times. You were about. I heard of your troubles." Walker looked around and started to move away. "Thing is, what happened to you is just plain commonplace anymore. They're killin' everybody that don't have a topknot and eagle feather."

Sean had a sudden thought. "You say you came out of Yellowstone? There's a friend of mine named Johnson. He and his woman were headed that way."

Walker nodded, turning his horse. "Yeah, I saw them at a rendezvous. Good folks." He shook his head. "I don't know why anyone would bring a decent woman around a bunch of randy trappers. She's a looker and he had a couple of fights over it, though it was mostly drunks. He cut 'em up pretty bad. I never heard of anything she did to bring it on, though. Far as I know, they're still ok."

Reaching out to stop the man, Sean said, "Don't run off. Do you know of a better way to cross the river? When we brought furs down the river on barges, we usually bypassed Chouteau's and went on down to

Saint Louis. I'm not familiar here."

Walker looked at him a moment. "Well, you can't swim it. Your horse would drown and you along with it. I might know a man with a flatboat that can take us across. If we can convince him, that is. He's a mile or so up the river."

"Friend of yours?" Sean asked as he fell in behind Walker's pack animals.

Walker spoke over his shoulder, between lightning flashes and thunder. "Didn't say that. He deals in things he accidentally finds along the river. Sometimes he finds whole keelboats just drifting along. If he has space on a boat for us, don't pay him until you get to the other side. If you get my drift."

Sean didn't reply, wondering if he should look for another way on his own. But the mountain man seemed honest enough.

"Oh," Walker continued, turning his head again so Sean could hear. "I wouldn't touch the women there, either. You can bet some of them ain't had a bath since I was there the last time. One of them gave me a gift I like to never got rid of."

He laughed and followed Walker and his pack animals up the trail. He had known many trappers. They were all solitary to a fault, but once they had company and loosened up a little, you couldn't shut them up with anything less than a war party busting out of the trees.

A half hour later, they walked their animals out of the scrub brush and down a slope toward the river. It was a grassy bank, with four cabins fronting the river and a flatboat tied to a short pier. Planks went from the boat to the shore, and some men struggled as they tried to roll barrels into the boat.

He looked the area over carefully. "I don't see much sign of traffic here. It's hardly even muddy. You'd think everyone would be trying to cross here."

"Yeah, well there's a lesson in that."

Walker paused and reloaded his Kentucky rifle, placing a piece of oilskin over the powder. "If your powder ain't dry, I'd do the same. These folks are friendly as long you keep your guard up."

Sean's rifle was in a beaded buckskin sheath. His habit was to recharge the weapon every morning, and it was ready now. He also had a musket looped over his saddle horn. A thin, greased membrane to keep it dry covered the pan and striker, but he wouldn't stake his life on it. His fighting knife and tomahawk were on his belt.

He grinned at the trapper. "Well now, we'll just have to make sure they stay friendly, won't we?"

A swarthy man with a raggedy beard walked out of the first building and stood under a porch so makeshift it looked like the weight of the rain would collapse the whole structure. He was dressed in baggy pants and shirt, knee-length leather boots, and had a red cap on his head. Four men came out and spread out behind him. All were armed, but didn't look too serious about it.

Sean swung his rifle to cover the men as Walker spoke. "How's it goin', McGarry?"

McGarry pushed his little hat back on his head. "Jim Walker! You made it another year. I figured your hair would be hangin' from a pole by now. Get down my friend — we'll have a jug of rum to celebrate another year." He clapped his hands and several women came out to stand on the porch of the next cabin over. "I'll bet it's been a while since you've had a woman, eh? These are young and fresh."

Walker lowered his rifle and seemed to waver. "Well, now. . . ."

Sean nudged Thunder up beside him. From what he could see through the rain, none of them looked young or fresh. "Jim, remember the gift."

Walker gave a shudder. "I know, I know. I

pissed blood for a week the last time. It felt like someone jammed a hot poker up —"

"Yeah, I got it." Sean laughed.

"And just who are you?" McGarry's voice was rough as he stared at Sean's rifle barrel tracking his belly button. "Why'd you interfere between me and my friend?"

"The name's Sean MacLeod, and we're looking for passage to the other side of the river." He looked pointedly at the man and lied. "And I promised his momma I'd look after him."

One of his men leaned up and whispered in McGarry's ear and Sean watched the man turned a curious shade of grey. "Heard of you. None of it good." He waved his arm at Walker. "Besides, he ain't got a momma and probably don't know his daddy."

Walker moved his horse a little closer to the blustering McGarry. "Don't let your mouth get you in trouble. So, how about it? I see your barge is about empty. Same price as before?"

Looking at Walker's furs, the avarice was plain in McGarry's eyes. "The river is pretty high, right now. It'll be hard to get across. Why don't you wait here a couple of days and relax a little?"

"In a couple of days it'll be higher. How much?" Sean was getting impatient. The men spread out a little, waiting for a sign from their boss, and there may have been movement by the other buildings.

"Twenty dollars."

"What?" Walker's voice cracked. "That's a couple of beaver."

McGarry smirked, thinking they would be broke. He could see Walker hadn't sold his furs. "In gold."

Walker was starting to cuss when Sean said, "It's a deal."

McGarry stepped forward with his hand out.

"You'll be paid on the other side." Sean pointed toward the building he'd seen the movement in. "And you make sure that person in the building yonder doesn't take a shot at us. I'll have your head on a stick if it happens."

McGarry stared at them a moment, and then grinned. He waived his hand toward the river. "Bah! Damned woodsrunners."

As he watched Walker dismount and lead his horse and pack animals down to the loading boards, Sean rode up to the barge and turned Thunder toward McGarry's men. "I'll just sit here and enjoy the rain while you get your pack animals loaded, Jim. Just to keep everything honest."

The boat was loaded and they untied from

the pier. At the last minute, McGarry came running down and jumped onto the boat.

"For a twenty-dollar gold piece, that bastard on the sweep probably wouldn't come back."

"You're so trusting." Walker laughed, trying to hold his horse steady. "It's a wonder you can sleep at night."

The crossing went smoothly and they unloaded on the other side. On the bank of the river, Sean handed McGarry his gold piece. The expression on his face was that of a man looking at a beautiful woman, a woman he just had to have.

"That was twenty dollars each."

"Not likely." Sean's voice was hard.

Before the man could back up, Sean grabbed him by the shirtfront. "Just a word of warning, McGarry. If I am robbed, you'd better make sure they kill me. Anything happens and I'll come for you. I don't think you're near as tough as the Blackfoot."

They watched as the man scurried back to his barge. "Think he'll try something, Jim?"

"Nah." Walker snorted, glancing up the clearing skies. "He's a sure thing operator. Oh, he'll steal from you quick enough. But he won't put himself in danger to do it."

The post bustled with activity. French and

American trappers mingled with Osage and Pawnee Indians. There were more tribes mingled together than he'd ever seen.

Walker tried to explain where they all lived. "The Osage live from here on south. Stay clear of them. They're bigger than most other Indians and touchy. I've heard they hide their women if a stranger comes calling and don't allow marriage outside their tribe. Mighty religious too. Them Pawnee over there come from west of here, along with the Kansa tribes." He laughed. "When you look at it, there's about as many people hereabouts as there are in the big cities back east. They're just more scattered out."

Avoiding the mud, they approached the buildings of the post from the back, moving along the bottom of a limestone bluff. A man stepped from the main building holding a long rifle. "What's your business here?"

Sean spoke up. "I'm looking for any of the Chouteau family. They're holding some goods for me, sent by Angus MacLeod."

The man turned and spoke to someone inside. A dapper looking young man stepped out to greet them, wiping his hands on a towel and speaking to the other man. "Arnold, those last furs were still green. We'll have to dock the owner just for the mess."

Almost in the same breath, he spoke to them. "You're Sean MacLeod? I'm Francois Chouteau. Welcome to our post. You're very welcome here. Look, I don't mean to be abrupt, but we're very busy right now. I'm sure you understand, knowing who you are." He pointed toward a building built back against the bluff. "There's a corral there, and feed for your horse. There's food inside and you can rest. I'll call for you this afternoon."

Sean nodded. "My friend here is Jim Walker. He has some furs to sell."

"We know Mister Walker." He motioned and the first man walked up to take the pack animals. "We'll unload these for you. Then we'll bring the animals to the corral. They'll be safe with us."

With that whirlwind conversation, Chouteau spun on his heel and went back into the building.

"Well, that was easy." Walker said. "I usually have to cool my heels out front with the rest of the riff-raff. Thanks, friend."

Aspen and a towering oak shaded the corral. They turned in their horses and made sure there was feed and water for them. Sean took an old blanket and rubbed down Thunder with it. The horse nuzzled into his shoulder. He never should have started feeding the horse apples.

An old Indian came out and spoke to him in stilted English. "I do this."

"No, he's used to me." He didn't want to lose his horse and was used to caring for Thunder himself. "I'll do it."

The old Indian stood as tall as his bent and broken frame would let him. "No steal. This is Palouse. Nez Perce horse." The old man spoke proudly and rubbed Thunder between his ears, which was about as far up as he could reach. "I take good care."

Walker was putting a feedbag on his roan and turned to the Indian. "What about mine?"

The old man gave a snort of derision, and then pointedly ignored Walker and his horse.

Walker laughed. "Don't worry about your horse. The old man's Nez Perce and works for the post. He'll take care of him."

Inside the long building, tables and benches filled the front of the room. The tables were all of twenty feet long and made from small trees split in half. The rough cut was probably done with a hand-turned blade at a sawmill and then smoothed by thousands of buckskin-clad elbows. Sean thought it would take ten men to bring in one table. As they sat, an Indian woman came out carrying plates of meat and pan-fried bread. Another came with pewter cups and a large jug. Both men were famished and immediately pulled small, pointed knives and attacked the food.

"Damn buffalo probably died of old age before they cut it up," Walker complained while reaching for the jug. He poured some into a cup and smelled it. "It's Flip." He turned the cup up and drained it. "Better watch this stuff. It tastes like it's mostly rum and short on beer and sugar. We'll wake up with a skull-buster and not know where we are."

Sean was only paying half attention, watching instead the Indian women.

The older woman stopped for a moment at a window facing the corral. The rain had slowed to a soft drizzle and all the shutters were open to let in the cool air. Sean glanced out his window and saw the old man standing at the head of Thunder, apparently speaking to the horse.

Just as he gazed back at the woman, her expression softened and she muttered, "Palouse."

When she glanced back at Sean, he thought she gave him a look of respect, and maybe gratitude before she returned to the kitchen.

A young woman went outside, and a few

moments later, the sound of a bell ringing drifted through the window. Soon their peace and quiet shattered as men stomped through the doorway for the noon meal. Several Indian women bustled about with plates of food and jugs for drink. A young-looking girl came to their table and spoke to Sean. He immediately noticed she wasn't included in the normal hand grabbing and boisterous jokes that normally went on in a tavern or eatery.

"There are rooms in back for you to rest, if you wish. I am to take care of you until Mister Chouteau sends for you."

"Why?"

"All my people know the stories of the Ghostrider, and we will take care of you. The Nez Perce and Blackfoot have fought many battles." She glanced at Jim. "Is this man your friend?" When Sean nodded, his head swimming from his third mug of flip, she walked away and said over her shoulder. "Please follow me."

In the back of the building were rooms with a single bed in each. At his cursory glance when they arrived, the building hadn't looked large enough to have sleeping quarters. The one she stopped at also had a tub filled with water and a new set of buckskins lay on the bed. Sean had a moment's thought that he didn't feel all that raggedy and dirty. Unlike some trappers and keelboaters, he actually hit the water with a bar of soap at least once a week.

"This room is for you." The girl stood with her hands clasped together and looked a little unsure of herself. "I will help you."

She wasn't beautiful like Angie, but she was very pretty. Her hair was brushed and long, and shone like a crow's wing. She had a clean smell to her that brought back memories of better times that he didn't want to visit. Her black eyes looked at him steadily, with no expression on her face except a smile. Inwardly, he groaned. It'd been nearly a year since he'd been with Angie or any other woman. Between getting over her death, and the feud with the Blackfoot, that part of him had just turned off.

Although still slightly addled from the flip, he didn't think this was normal behavior for an Indian girl he'd just met.

"Look, I really appreciate it, but I can take my own bath. And please, thank Mister Chouteau for the new clothes."

She shook her head at him. "Not from Chouteau. Chouteau not give anything free. My grandfather has much happiness taking care of your horse. It's been a long time since we had a Palouse like yours. It brings back many memories for him and also for my mother." She smiled at him again, and then pouted. "I would think most men would be honored to have me help them. Am I not pleasing to you?"

"Oh, you're pleasing. I'm just a little drunk and more than a little confused."

He watched her flounce away, obviously angry when he declined her offer and sent her back. Walker just shook his head.

Suddenly Sean was grumpy as a bear with a sore paw. "And just how long have you been standing there watching that little show? I can't believe she'd do that so easily. What kind of morals do they have?"

Leaning against the doorframe, Walker laughed at him. "That, my friend, wasn't usual or normal. I'll bet they're saying the same thing about you and probably wondering if you don't like girls."

"I don't understand."

"That's your problem, Sean. You're trying to over think this. If you go to France, things are different. Go to England? Things are different. Hell, Saint Louis seems like another world. Even the tribes are different. She wants to give you a gift, boy. You don't have to know why. All you need to know is she's willing. Maybe she just likes your looks. I heard an old saying once. And it works for trying to understand Indians, or actually women in general. You'll notice I lump them both together. A web is normal for the spider, but chaos for the fly."

He glanced at the man. "What are you, a school teacher? Besides, Professor Walker, I don't always have to be the fly."

As he was closing his door, Walker said. "Do you think I was born with a beaver trap in my hand? I wasn't always a trapper, you know. Let's get some rest."

The water wasn't warm, but fell far short of the coldness of a mountain stream. It relaxed him to the point he barely made it out of the tub before he collapsed naked on the bed. He just rolled a blanket around him and went to sleep. For the first time in months, he slept a dreamless sleep.

He awoke with light streaming through the east window and what felt like someone beating a drum inside his head. That was a hell of a drink. When he moved, the lump under the covers with him moaned and sat up. Her tousled, long black hair barely covered her young breasts. As he watched, she rose naked from the bed, and with a yawn and smile took a rag to the tub that was still full of water and soaked it. Giggling, she tossed him the wet rag. "Clean yourself. You smell of sweat."

Throwing a simple, flowered dress over her body in one fluid motion, she leaned over and kissed him on the mouth before he could object.

What the hell? He took the rag and, standing by the tub, dutifully gave himself a rag bath.

He was still standing naked and drying off when she came back into the room with a new set of clothes. "I found out the clothes we sent you would not fit. You're much larger than I thought you'd be." Again, the giggle as he tried to cover himself. "Much larger." She tossed him the clothes she brought. "These will do."

A few minutes later, dressed in new buckskins, he found Walker sitting out in the dining area nursing a cup of coffee. The man could hardly drink behind his wide grin.

"Have a good rest?"

"I thought Chouteau was going to send for me."

"Oh, he did." Walker smirked. "You were busy, so I told them you were being measured for a new set of clothes and that we'd see him sometime today. Why? You in a big hurry?"

The women came out with heaping plates of meat and eggs. When the younger girl came to him, she brushed him with her hip and laughed.

Flashes of memory from the night before assailed him. "I'd at least like to know your name."

She turned to look at him and for a moment, he couldn't read her expression. Regret? Sadness? "You may call me Willow. I'll bring more food if you want it. You have big appetite."

He looked up at Walker and was surprised the man had his hand on the older woman's backside.

"Ah, man. You didn't. . . ."

"Hey, these folks are friendly. If this is the reception you get everywhere you go, I'm going to be your friend a long time."

He shook his head and instantly regretted it. "I just wish I could remember it."

An hour later, they were ushered into an office at the back of the trading post. Francois Chouteau shook both their hands. "So, young Sean. You look well rested. Have you enjoyed your stay so far?"

While Jim snickered and rolled his eyes, Sean said. "What I can remember of it. I think someone spiked my rum."

"It packs a wallop if you're not used to it. I assume there are no ill effects from the night. I'll have no one say you didn't have your wits about you when we do business. No? Well, to business then. Mister Walker, the same consideration as usual?"

"Yup." Walker shrugged. "Just float me some spending money and I'll take the rest on a letter of credit. I'll get my supplies when I go back to the North Country."

"Fair enough. Now, Sean, we have a lot of business to discuss. If you don't mind, I'd like Mister Walker to stay as a witness so I can dispense my obligations."

"Obligations?" He glanced at Walker. "I was just told to come and pick up some furs, if I decided to come this way. What obligation would you have to me?"

Chouteau shuffled papers. "In the past, I've not always been successful. Angus gave me a hand up when I needed it. He also shipped a great number of furs and castoreum through here for which he was never paid. The last courier from MacLeod's post instructed me to turn over all his monies and belongings to you upon demand."

"How much are we talking?"

Chouteau consulted a ledger in front of him. "It amounts to well over twenty thousand dollars."

Sean went quiet and Walker gasped behind him. "That's a lot of money."

"It is, indeed. So, what are your intentions? If you want it in furs to take to Saint Louis, I can provide some guards and a keelboat. You might get a better price there. Or, like Mister Walker has done, I can give you a letter of credit until you decide what to do."

"Man," Walker said wondrously, taking off his hat and running his fingers through his hair. "When I saw you on that skinny Palouse and your butt showing through your pants, I didn't figure you for being worth a plugged nickel. Hell, from what I've heard, you were lucky to get away from the Upper Missouri with all your hair."

"And yet, you befriended me, Walker. That was a fine thing to do and I appreciate it. You helped me when I needed it and I'll not forget it."

Chouteau was waiting impatiently, drumming his fingers on the table, when Sean finally made his decision. "I'm thinking of setting up a store of my own. I've talked to a few people about it and this country is starting to fill up. But I don't want to settle along the big rivers or compete with the big companies like yours. I've heard good things about the White River country, south of here. I think I'll try my hand there."

"All right, then." Chouteau replied. "In

the morning I'll have three pack mules loaded with goods of trade. If you'll allow me, I'll send you out with the things I know you will need. I've had some experience at that. The trade goods will be for dealing with the Indians. It takes many gifts, and they will appreciate good quality. When you get settled somewhere, let me know and I'll help stock your trading post." He thought a moment, rubbing his chin. "In fact, I might be interested in giving you some help in that regard. We've been thinking of expanding again."

Walker, standing by the door and out of Chouteau's line of sight, was vigorously shaking his head.

"All right, Mister Chouteau, I'll think about it. But while I appreciate the offer, I expect to do this on my own. I don't want to be beholden to anyone. That way if I fail, it's all on me."

"Of course, it will be as you wish." Chouteau rose, perfunctorily shook their hands, and abruptly left the room. They could hear him calling for people as soon as he entered the main store.

Walker watched the Frenchman through the door. "Well, he's a fidgety thing, ain't he?"

They went outside and strolled back

toward the corral and bunkhouse. Sean glanced back at the post. "Mister Chouteau seems to be a bit controlling."

Walker laughed. "A bit controlling? You think all this just happened? We show up out of the woods and they treat us like kings. All we can eat, fresh clothes, and a real bed to sleep in. Do you think a woman to warm our beds was an accident, and a clean woman at that? Not like those whores at McGarry's. His thumb is on everything for miles around, and he owes you a lot of money. I'm thinking money isn't something he likes to give that easy. I'm thinking he wants you beholden to him."

"Well, I can see all that, except for the women. They're Nez Perce. The girl Willow said it's her grandfather that provided all of that, just for getting to take care of Thunder."

Walker just shook his head. "No, I'm thinkin' you're wrong. They like your horse and give you a gift of new buckskins. Send you the girl? I'm not buying that."

Sean stopped and slapped him on the shoulder. "It doesn't really matter. I'm just a woodsrunner like you. I always will be."

"Yeah, right. Chouteau never gave me the time of day before this. Nope, I'm just thankin' my lucky stars we met up like we did." Walker smiled at him and then rolled his eyes in laughter. "I'm just baskin' in your glory."

The man's laughter was infectious and Sean couldn't help but join in. "Go to hell, Walker."

They spent the rest of the day sitting around telling stories and swapping lies with trappers and traders. Many of the men were selling furs at the post, and then going on down the river to Saint Louis to spend their money.

Sean was curious. "Why not spend it here?"

"On what?" Walker waved his arms around in a circle. "Saint Louie's got every kind of trouble a man wants to get into. You can really bust loose down there. We'll be gettin' a group together soon and you should come with us."

Sean just smiled, shaking his head. "I've had enough excitement and trouble to last a lifetime. All I want is peace and quiet. Thanks anyway, but I'll have to pass. Besides, there'll be enough flip on that boat you won't know when you get there."

He soon left the impromptu party and found his room again. Later, he came to when Willow came into his room and shucked out of her dress. Sean tried to protest, but her fingers covered his mouth. Moments later, her mouth replaced her hand and no more words were needed. Later, as he drifted off to sleep he thought hitting the trail would be more restful.

Sean staggered into the eating room as the first sunlight peeked through the windows. Walker, as usual, sat at a table nursing a cup of coffee in his big hands.

"Man, you sleep late. You look like warmed over death. With you gettin' up so late in the morning it's a wonder it didn't take you a year to make it here from the Upper Missouri."

"Go to hell."

"You keep tellin' me that, but I ain't moved yet. See? Look behind you. I've been settin' here for hours, but they wouldn't feed me until you showed up. I damned near starved."

Willow and her mother came in with fry bread, venison, and eggs. Sean noticed Willow didn't look much better than he did and was strangely pleased.

Walker cleared his throat and broke into his thoughts. "His happiness, the exalted Mister Chouteau, was here earlier. You know, when most normal folks were already up." Handing Sean a folded, soft leather pouch, he said. "That's got your letter of credit in it. I wouldn't lose that if I was you. If you come back without it, I doubt he'll remember your name."

Sean looked in the pouch and, leaving the credit document inside, withdrew a single sheet of paper. Walker's eyes widened as he handed him the paper.

"What's this?" Walker read the few lines on the paper, and then looked up at Sean. "You're giving me free access on your letter of credit? On demand?" The man shook his head. "Are you crazy?"

"Look at it this way." Sean grinned at him. "Now, he has to keep a record just in case you come asking. Just think of it as insurance in case something happens to me."

"But you don't even know me."

"You gonna steal from me? Take it and run?" Sean shook his head. "I don't know you very well. Hell, I don't know you at all, but I know your type. When we had the post, Angus MacLeod would meet a man for the first time and tell him yes or no. Credit or no credit. Stay or leave. I learned at his side. Face it, Walker. You're an honest man. You'll just have to deal with it."

After he finished breakfast, he left a still-speechless Walker and went outside, only to stop dead in his tracks. Before him were twenty Indians forming a gauntlet line. At a glance, he saw these were warriors, not the usual bunch that hung around the post looking for handouts. They were armed, but looked friendly enough. The old Nez Perce stood at the end of the line holding Thunder's reins.

But that old man had changed. Now he was tall and proud, with new buckskins and blanket. He wasn't the slumped over old man Sean had seen just two days before.

Saddled and bridled, Thunder looked ready for the trail. The two-day rest hadn't put any meat on his bones, but he'd picked up a lot of energy. His winter coat had been brushed away to leave a clean, white sheen. They'd braided his mane with small feathers in the knots. Sean wasn't sure, but he thought the horse looked a little embarrassed.

Beyond the horse were three pack mules loaded with his goods. The older mule with the grey muzzle looked at him and bared his teeth, shaking its head and snorting foam. He heard soft laughter of sympathy from the warriors behind him.

The old man stepped forward and started speaking in his language and with signs. Sean just shook his head, looking around for Walker. As the old man continued to speak, Walker would nod and make a reply in return. Finally, he stopped talking.

"What'd he say?"

"Oh, he said a lot. You scare the hell out of me the way you make friends. The old man's name is Buffalo Horn. Hell, I think half the warriors on the plains are named Buffalo sumthin' or other. The rest of these warriors are in his clan. You're kind of a hero to them. Seems they have a real dislike for Blackfoot and the Bloods in particular. They know of your story and how many Blackfoot you've put away."

"How many I've put away? I don't even know that. I've never counted."

Walker smiled. "That's all right. I gave them a big number for you. Look at them. They're impressed."

Sean looked at the warriors, smiling at them while talking to Walker. "You lied?"

"Well, I wouldn't exactly say I lied. That's a mortal sin. But since you don't know how many, any number could be the truth. Oh, and one more thing you should know. That brave standing over there next to your little gal Willow don't seem half as happy about you as the rest of them. I'd steer clear of that, if I was you."

The men were all looking at him, clearly expecting something. "Interpret for me,

Walker. And try to stay as close to the truth as you can.

"I have known many tribes. My adopted father is Scottish, from across the great water. My slain wife was French" — he heard Walker say *français* — "I am allied to the Cree nation. Now, I am proud to call the Nez Perce my brothers."

When Walker translated, the men all shouted their approval.

Sean continued. "My brothers will receive a new knife and blanket from Chouteau. This is my gift to you." He turned to Thunder and pulled his spare fighting knife and scabbard from his bedroll. Turning, he presented the knife to Buffalo Horn. "This I give to Buffalo Horn for his friendship. Kaini blood stains the blade. It's fitting you should have it."

His men and family all gathered around, looking at the prize.

"Hear me." Sean waited until he had their attention. "You know of my feud with the Blackfoot. Much killing has happened. Too much killing and many lodges mourn the loss of their sons. It's at an end. I have gone away from their land and the Ghostrider is no more. I only wish to live in peace."

Sean turned back to Thunder and prepared to leave. Buffalo Horn spoke to

Walker, and handed him a folded piece of oilskin.

Everyone drifted away while Sean checked the loads on the mules. Walker came up and handed the oilskin to Sean.

"They heard you were going south, so they got their heads together with some Osage and drew you a map of the rivers. It might come in handy."

Sean shook Walker's hand. "Come with me, Jim. I could use the help."

"Nah. I'm for cuttin' loose in Saint Louis. I dreamt of it all winter."

"Make sure you don't get your cuttin' by some gambler while you're having so much fun. Sometimes the dream is better than the actual fact." Sean grinned at him. "And, don't pick up any 'gifts' from the ladies, either."

Sean had mounted when Walker put his hand up to stop him. "One thing Buffalo Horn told me. You be careful. They heard the Bloods are sending someone after you to put an end to the feud. Ever heard of a Buffalo Shield?"

"No. Although, it's like you said. I think every clan of the Blackfoot has someone named Buffalo Shield."

"Well, whoever this one is, he's some kind of medicine man or shaman and supposed to be poison mean. The old man was kind of spooked about it. You'd better watch your back trail."

"Thanks, Walker. Look, if you get tired of dodging hostiles and chasing beaver, look me up on the White River. We'll tip a jug of rum and tell a bunch of lies."

Walker just smiled and nodded. "Well, like the song says, if I don't get killed, I'll live till I die. I might just come and see ya."

With no more parting than that, they went their separate ways. It was the way of the mountain man. They would meet a friend in the wilderness, break bread, swap a few lies, and then go on their way. He truly hoped Walker would break that mold and come south.

Sean had just entered the woods, out of sight of the clearing when Buffalo Horn and Willow stepped onto the trail in front of him. He reined up and just stared at them. What the hell?

Buffalo Horn saw his discomfort and smiled at him. "Do not worry, Ghostrider. I'm not making you take my granddaughter with you. She already has a husband."

Sean dismounted from his horse and his mind was racing, wondering what this was all about. Finally, he just shook his head. "Then, what?"

Suddenly, Willow broke away from her grandfather's side and hugged Sean a moment, her face against his chest. Slowly, his arms went around her.

Her deep brown eyes were shiny with unshed tears as she kissed him on the cheek. "Thank you." Her voice was soft as her fingers lingered on his lips, keeping him from saying anything. She turned and walked back into the woods. As she turned to wave, he saw the young brave who'd been with her earlier step out to meet her.

Buffalo Horn cleared his throat to get Sean's attention. "They have been together many seasons, with no children. She could take another husband, and he another wife, but there is much love between them. She is in her fertile time. Now, the seed of the Ghostrider is in her. It may grow, or it may not. The Great Spirit will decide this."

Sean had to make a physical effort to close his mouth. Of all the things he could think of, only one came to mind. He'd been put out to stud the brood mare and didn't even realize it. "But, why me? Surely there's someone in your own clan you could turn to?"

The old man shrugged and smiled. "For her to take another Nez Perce man would only cause conflict in the clan. Our men are very proud, maybe too much so. If she has a child from your seed, think of the warrior he would be. Think of the joining of the mighty Ghostrider and the Nez Perce princess. Songs will be sung of this child."

Still befuddled, Sean managed a smile. "What if it's a girl?"

"We have heard the songs of the Blackfoot when they fought the Battle of Cross Timbers. It is said the mother was as great a warrior as the father, maybe even stronger." The old man shrugged. "It will be a great song either way."

Still confused, Sean extended his hand in friendship. "I don't understand this and don't know whether to wish you and her luck, or not. If a child is born, I hope you live long enough to see your dream. Either way, I'd like word if a child is born. I'll make no claim, but I'd want to know."

"It shall be so."

Sean wondered what Walker would have said about him being put out to stud. He could see the smirk now. Mounting, he turned Thunder and his pack mules south to pick up the old Indian trace that would lead him to the White River country.

Four

Sean MacLeod's eyes opened in darkness from a troubled sleep, wondering what small sound had alerted him. His fighting knife came to his hand like a well-worn glove, ready to meet whatever danger lurked in the dark.

The night wind rustled through the leaves above him, but left no breeze on the forest floor. Thunder grumbled in the distance, and he pondered staying in his blankets, but sleep would not come back. Not this night.

Trusting his senses, he rolled over on his blanket, coming to one knee, and then rose quietly to his feet. Not hearing anything out of the ordinary, he relaxed and called on the one thing that sustained him through the year of a spirit trail called revenge. Calm fury, waiting for the bloodletting.

When the attack came, he faced the wrong way. The point of a knife swept through his buckskin shirt and cut a shallow, burning gash along his ribs. Desperately, he spun on his heel away, making a level swipe with his own fighting knife. The fine steel cut through the air, but found nothing to slake its thirst for blood. He took three quick steps away and sank to one knee, trying to control the sound of his own breathing. The night was black as the bottom of a well and he heard no sound but his wildly thudding heart.

The night was a friend and he did not fear it. He knew the denizens of the forest, and he knew their habits and sound. He had to find his attacker and quickly. To be surprised again could be fatal. Methodically, he processed the sounds of the forest around him. Thunder and the mules were tethered in the trees a short distance away. They were awake and moving restlessly, but they'd given no alarm. Mules were usually better than dogs for sentry duty.

Once the first flurry of movement stopped, the night cautiously came alive. Forest creatures, not surprised by sudden death, would give the occurrence but a moment's notice. The owl he heard certainly didn't care. Within minutes, the raccoon he'd seen earlier in the evening would continue fishing for crawfish in the nearby stream, the fox would make rustling noises in the leaves trying to scare up a mouse, and deer would continue to graze in the glades of tall grass.

Running Elk crouched in the darkness of the clearing and shivered when he heard the owl. The owl hoot, a sign of death to his people, spoke of ghosts wandering in the night, unable to enter the spirit land. Why now? Whom did the owl want? Was it waiting for him, or his prey? The Indian shook off the bad thoughts. Either way, he was committed. Someone would die this night.

Earlier, the Indian had placed his lance and bow on the ground beyond the edge of the clearing, fearing the longer weapons would catch on the brush around him and give him away. He stood in the darkness, testing the sharpness of the blade with the thumb of his other hand, imagining he felt the warm blood of the Ghostrider. He wished he'd brought his spear. The last encounter was too close.

It had been a long journey with much waiting. Now that the time had come, the Indian was uncommonly impatient to continue the attack. He had stalked his prey on other nights, and could always tell by the sound of the man's breathing that he did not sleep sound. His quarry was always restless, tossing and turning, waking several times during the night. Thoughts of the Ghostrider lying there listening to the night had kept him from attacking.

This night had been different. The Ghostrider had stayed awake far into the evening, fighting his drowsiness. Finally, he seemed to fall into a deep, exhausted sleep.

All the warriors in his village knew of MacLeod, and had a deep respect for his fighting ability. The reasoning for a night attack was simple. Running Elk felt it was a foolish risk to confront MacLeod in broad daylight. It would be a mighty coup to kill him, even at night. A kill was a kill. Running Elk's village would cherish MacLeod's scalp.

The warrior was impatient for action, but at the same time felt reluctant about continuing the fight. Slowly, as the sun painted the first streaks in the eastern sky, fear trickled into his mind. Was the owl's call for him? No, it could not be . . . he'd drawn first blood.

The owl hooted again, but Sean's mind filtered out the normal sounds, knowing instinctively that the owl hoot was real. The air was humid and sticky and he longed to wipe the sweat from his face. He strained for the one small piece of noise that didn't fit . . . and finally heard it behind him and to his left. A small frown formed on his lips as his heart trip-hammered once again, and then settled to a steady beat. His assailant hadn't left.

Close upon the first thought came a second. Who? Not likely a white man, though he didn't completely discount the idea. He knew from experience that evil and death wore many colors.

He thought of the warning given by Buffalo Horn to his friend, Jim Walker. The warning was that the Blackfoot were sending a Medicine Man and great warrior to kill the hated Ghostrider. Was this the one?

Night winds rustled the leaves of the towering oak above him, slipping through the foliage with measured fingers. Coming closer, the thunderstorm growled beyond the trees, punctuated by a brief flare of light sifting through the forest.

The wind playing with the treetops did not extend itself to the ground but offered a scant breeze that brought the smell of the forest and a hint of rain. The slight wind lifted the oppressive heat.

He gripped the handle of his knife. He wanted to reach to his side, needed to assess the damage and gauge the amount of blood he was losing, but didn't dare. He didn't want slick blood on his hand, and the slight movement might be the one thing his attacker was waiting on.

He remained alert as he gripped his fighting knife firmly, cutting edge up, holding his elbows close to his body so his arms would protect against another thrust. Only a fool stabs downward with a knife. There are too many bones in the upper body, bones that could deflect the blade and give your enemy a chance. Better to hold the knife low, cutting edge up, and go for the soft parts.

He finally eased himself up from the ground. It was time to end this. Even a small amount of blood loss could weaken him and he didn't intend to give his attacker that advantage.

A stronger breeze started up, and he caught a strong scent in the darkness. An acrid and dangerous smell, one he knew well, sharp with wood smoke and tallow.

The night stayed quiet for a long time, but he didn't relax. He could feel it. Death was coming again. There was a slight rustle a few feet to his right that didn't follow the pattern of the wind. Knowing that anyone trying to see in the dark would have their eyes opened wide, he took a chance. Risking the noise, he picked up a handful of loose soil and leaves, instantly throwing it toward the sound with an underhand motion, spreading the dirt in a fine spray.

A sudden gasp came from the dark shadows as the soil found its mark. He lunged toward the sound. The Indian heard him coming and turned to grapple with him. They came together in a fumble of elbows and knives.

They strained against each other in the darkness, each trying to gain an advantage over the other. Each had the same idea as they cracked knees in an attempt to crush the other's groin.

The man lunged again and got his knifepoint tangled in Sean's buckskin shirt. He grabbed the man and hip-rolled him to the ground, losing him immediately in the darkness. Sean risked everything with a wide sweep of his blade, level with the ground and knee-high.

His blow caught the Indian coming up off the ground. His blade snagged a moment, and then cut deep into flesh. The man gave a hoarse scream and tried to roll away, a vague shadow on the ground. Sean followed relentlessly, not wanting to lose him again.

They came together in the center of the clearing, panting hard as they fought. He sensed something coming toward him and threw up his left arm, blocking the tomahawk as it came down in an overhead swing at his head. He countered by slashing upward with his blade.

Cold steel ripped into the Indian's belly. Sean felt the first resistance — the desperate and surprised hardening of stomach muscles trying to deny the knife its journey. Then, as the blade dove into soft flesh, the man's muscles surrendered. A gush of warm blood covered Sean's hand as he withdrew the knife.

The man slumped against him. The cloying odor of blood and sweat hovered between them. The Indian's breath came out in a sharp gasp of pain, and then changed to a long sigh, as his knife and tomahawk dropped from nerveless fingers. The Indian muttered something in a gurgling breath, but the words were never finished.

Clutching each other like lovers in the dark, Sean felt the life go out of the man, felt it when he gave it up. The Indian slipped limply through his grasp to the ground.

Trying to quiet his ragged breathing, he stepped away from the fallen man. Feeling his blanket against his feet, he picked it up and wrapped it around his shoulders. Holding his left arm against the wound in his side, he settled down to wait. He was sure the Indian was dead, but only a fool fiddles with a wounded man in the dark.

And he didn't know if this man was alone.

He sat shivering in the darkness under the tree, knowing he wouldn't sleep, and thinking of the dream he had the night before. The dreams were always the same, filled with fire and screaming, broken bodies sprawled in death, exploding him from sleep to leave him sweating and panting, standing in the middle of the night, searching for his enemies.

He had come to fear sleep, because of the dreams. The real fear wasn't of the dreams themselves, but of the anger and pain rekindled by the nightmares, and the realization he could easily return to the path he'd left behind. The dreams pulled at his spirit and pushed him toward a raging fire of hatred. And he did not want to go. . . .

Remembering the past months, he thought his anger would have gone away or at least abated. The struggle through the winter snow from the Upper Missouri River down to Kawsmouth took his mind off his troubles awhile. Making a new friend in Jim Walker and the brief, confusing, but pleasant interlude with Willow had helped, but the anger was still there. It lurked in his mind like a giant cat waiting to spring its trap. He reasoned the cat was his anger and his soul was the prey. The cat was constantly stalking and he didn't know how to break away.

He'd lived on hatred and anger. The Indians began calling him Ghostrider. They were right. He felt drained. Inside he felt dead. And tired. He was tired of the anger and the killing that gained him no relief. Tired of the emptiness in his mind. And most of all, tired of death.

He shifted his position under the tree, suddenly realizing he was sitting on a rock. He pulled it from under him, started to toss it toward the dead Indian, then put it gently beside him. There was no use making any more noise than necessary.

He thought he'd put the killing behind him. But although he couldn't be sure until daylight, there was another dead Blackfoot in the clearing. He leaned against the tree, wrapped in his blanket, thinking about the events of the last couple of days.

Two days ago, he rose before dawn, wolfing down a breakfast of cold fish and stanica, an Indian bread made of persimmon and corn. Finished with the loading of his pack animals, he paused to look at the bindings of the packs. Once satisfied nothing would fall off, he reached for his saddle and paused in mid-stride, frozen for a moment.

Beside it was a clearly defined footprint in the soft earth that hadn't been there when he'd put the saddle down.

He straightened slowly and gazed around, thinking about it. Now, that saddle was in the center of the clearing, a good fifteen feet from the edge of the trees. He gazed around again, mildly cursing to himself, and more than a little annoyed to think someone had sneaked into his camp right under his nose.

Someone? He wouldn't be more surprised if he looked up and saw fifty Osage pounding down on him and screaming for his hair. That was expected. But a lone man walking into his camp and then leaving undetected while he was nearby?

He shrugged, thinking he must have missed it previously. Although for the life of him he couldn't imagine missing that track, and if he hadn't missed it. . . .

The track was large, and dug in at the toes. It was a man's track, and he could assume the man was big, quick, and silent on his feet. The question was, who? He hadn't seen many people in the last couple of hundred miles after leaving Kawsmouth, trading rarely with the different tribes he encountered along the way when he needed supplies. Lost in thought, he tied his long blond hair in the back with a piece of rawhide, and slapped on his floppy hat. An enemy? Possible, but not likely. The Blackfoot were northern Indians and he hadn't heard of any traveling this far south. So, who? A friend would have stayed. An enemy would have attacked. *Strange.*

FIVE

In the grey, first light of dawn, Sean went to inspect the man he'd killed. Rifle in hand, he pushed the Indian's shoulder with a careful foot. When there was no response, he rolled the man over on his back. Sightless eyes stared past a sprinkling of dirt and leaves, never to see the canopy of leaves above.

He'd guessed right, it was a young Blackfoot brave. He cursed softly, remembering the mumbled words from the night before. They'd sounded familiar then, and the memory of them had an ominous ring now.

So, they were still sending warriors on the spirit trail. Would it never end? How far would he have to travel to end this? His anger toward them was gone, but their anger was still hot. In addition, there were a lot more of them than he could take care of. Through the many battles he'd fought, anger had carried him until skill took over.

Skill couldn't last forever. There would always be someone bigger and stronger coming up the trail. He wasn't foolish enough to think he could defeat all the Bloods in battle. When anger and skill run out, you have to rely on luck . . . and luck is a fickle mistress who laughs at a man's feeble attempts at life.

The dead Indian, a young man, bore the handsome features of his tribe. There'd be someone at his village waiting for his return, waiting to mourn when he didn't. The cycle of vengeance needed to end.

To anyone watching the trails, the full head of black hair and long-sleeved buckskins, even in the summer heat, would have given him away as a stranger in this forest. He caught a glimpse of color under the man and moved him enough to pull it out. He held the red cloth in his hands a moment, and then gripped it tightly in his fist, shaking his head.

The Bloods. The elite clan, seasoned warriors all, sworn to never surrender, and as fighting men there were none better. The traditional red sash hanging from the Indian's waist was their badge of honor. It was their pride to go first into battle, and to stay behind to cover the retreat, when the other warriors had to flee. And it was still their pride to try and kill the Ghostrider.

He allowed himself a moment of thanksgiving. He was extremely lucky. The brave must have traveled by night as he stalked Sean, otherwise the local Osage would've picked him off. The Osage, jealous of their hunting grounds, guarded their boundaries with their lives . . . and the bodies of their enemies.

Earlier, while waiting for dawn, he'd convinced himself he'd been the victim of a random attack, that some Indian couldn't resist a chance to pick off a lone white man. His wealth of trade goods and horses would be tempting to many a man, red or white. Now he knew better. To the warrior this had been personal. And, he admitted to himself, with good reason.

After he killed so many of the Blood clan, they started sending their young men on a medicine trail of vengeance. To prove his manhood, a young Blackfoot would seek out and try to kill the hated Ghostrider. It had become a quest for them, and there didn't seem to be any lack of volunteers. For a long time, he had looked forward to the game. But as old Bear Hunter had predicted, the killing rage had worn off, leaving in its place a tiredness of mind that was hard to shake off.

Before last night, he thought the hunting would end when he passed from their territory.

He circled the clearing, looking for sign. A ring of forest fern and low bushes surrounded the open space, each plant fighting for its share of sunlight that filtered through the canopy of leaves in the hardwood forest.

He looked for anything out of place — crushed stems on the fern, grass bent the wrong way, or scuff marks on the bark of trees. He didn't find anything until he looked at the base of a honeysuckle bush and found a set of tracks. It was a good place. The bush was high enough someone could stand and not be backlit by moonlight if it happened to peek out of the clouds. A man had stood there, not moving. One track pointed toward the forest. Searching further, he found one more . . . and then there was nothing. Not a track, nor a broken twig. Nothing.

Hands on hips, he stood a long time staring into the forest. It appeared to be the same track he'd seen in his camp two days before. Now, who . . . ? His thoughts went back to Buffalo Horn's warning. This young brave sure wasn't some kind of legendary warrior.

Well, hell.

▪ ▪ ▪ ▪

Later, Sean carried the dead Indian to the burial platform he had built of young saplings at the edge of the clearing. He wrapped the man in a blanket, and heaved him up onto the platform. As he straightened the body, he placed the Indian's weapons next to him. It was tempting to take the bow for himself, but he preferred his own English-style longbow. The disadvantage of his bow was its length, about six feet, which was hard to use in the confines of the brush and trees, but it suited him. He loved the power of the English longbow.

He hadn't found the dead man's horse, or he would have tied it to the platform. At least, for a while. If he found it, he would take the extra horse with him. It didn't make sense to waste a good animal for a dead man.

Returning to camp, he finished loading the pack animals, wishing once more he'd left Old Grey at Kawsmouth. Pete and Tom were normal mules who just seemed to want to do their jobs everyday if he would be nice enough to stake them in a nice meadow at night. Old Grey was another story. He was large for a mule, standing nearly sixteen hands, crooked as a Virginia fence, and a slow starter in the mornings.

Dodging his teeth, Sean stepped away when Old Grey tried to stomp on his foot. "We don't have much farther to travel, old boy, and I'm gonna sell you to some unsuspecting settler to pull a plow. See how you like that."

He petted Thunder a moment after he saddled him. The warhorse given to him by Bear Hunter was tired and gaunt, but still had the spirit to go all day. That was another decision he had to make . . . he needed to find a place soon. They all needed a place to rest.

As he gathered his weapons, he checked his loads, made sure his knife and hatchet were riding free at his waist, and then turned and waited. The mules had been looking down the trail for the last minute or so, and he heard the snort of a horse in the distance. To run would be useless, and besides, he was in a black mood anyway.

The war ponies of the Osage shuffled through the long grass as they approached the camp, nostrils flaring and ears forward. He felt a moment's envy at the sight of ponies trained for war like the chargers rode by knights of old, and probably fought against by his ancestors. Their slashing hooves could cut a man to pieces, and their bite inflicted terrible damage. But they were southern horses and didn't have the size of his mount. They'd not do well in the snows of the north. He didn't turn to look, but by the sound of Thunder blowing behind him, his horse had rolled his eyes in contempt.

There were eight warriors, and as they stopped before him, they spread out in a rough skirmish line of restless horses, feathered lances, and hard eyes. Two of them broke off immediately to look at the burial platform. The remaining men waited in silence.

He let them stare, holding his rifle casually across his chest. Only two of them had flintlock muskets, the rest held bows already set with arrows. The muskets were the least dangerous. Any of the Plains Indians of the North Country could shoot twelve arrows a minute with accuracy. He didn't figure the Osage were any different.

They were huge men, all well over six feet, their heads plucked bald, except for a scalp lock in the back. A single eagle feather adorned the roach of hair, and gold rings glittered as they hung in the lobes of their ears. All were naked except for a loincloth, and each of their bodies showed the scars of battle. Only one of the men wore moccasins.

His mouth turned dry. These were seasoned warriors. Only an idiot would lowrate these men.

They looked over his horse and one of the men muttered something about Palouse, but it came out as a Poloosa.

One of the Indians started toward the pack animals, a man with close-set eyes and a twisted look about him. Sean let the muzzle of his rifle point toward the man's chest. The Osage stopped, sneering at him with open hatred on his face . . . and still not a spoken word.

His stomach churned like a water wheel. The warhorses of the Osage stomped restlessly, anticipating the fight to come. Even the Osage horses seemed to hate intruders upon their land.

The two men returned from the platform, spoke softly, and shrugged their shoulders as the Osage sitting slightly in front of the others questioned them. The man finally walked his horse forward, guiding it with his knees and leaving a dark trail in the dew-covered grass of the clearing. He stopped a few feet in front of Sean.

"Did you kill him?" the Indian asked in a rich baritone voice.

Sean's eyebrows went up at his use of English. It never ceased to amaze him how Indians could learn multiple languages with ease. He answered simply. "I did."

At this admission, the Osage warriors surged forward, but stopped short when their leader raised his hand. He gazed calmly at Sean. He seemed more curious than angry.

"My warriors would kill you, to avenge the death of our brother from far away. But there is something I don't understand. You put him on the platform, his face to the rising sun, according to Osage custom. His weapons are with him, to use in the afterlife, and you didn't maim or torture him. I would know why."

Sean shrugged, watching one of the warriors trying to move up on his left again. If they thought he was distracted, they were wrong.

"The young warrior attacked me in the night." He lifted his shirt with his left hand, showing the cut on his side. "He made a good try." Thinking to spook them a little, he added, "The owl had already spoken for the young brave." He swung his rifle. "If that man doesn't stop, I'm going to shoot him right off his horse."

The Osage leader turned, and barked a

command at the warrior. The man abruptly reined his horse in, and returned to the group, an angry expression on his face. It was the narrow-eyed one again, the one with the permanent sneer on his face.

"As I said," he continued. "The young warrior attacked me. We fought as men. The Great Spirit decides who will live, and who will die. I buried him in this manner because it's a way I'd heard of Indian burials, and the only honor I can give him." He shrugged. "It may not be his way. I don't know. I left his weapons so he may use them in the afterlife and did not maim him because, when we meet again, I would greet him as a brother and not as an enemy."

"You know the Osage way?"

"I am Sean MacLeod of the Northwest Fur Company. My family trades with many tribes. We know of the mighty Osage."

The Indian looked at him a long moment. "We also know the name of MacLeod. Your people deal fairly with the Indian, not like other traders. I have also heard your trading post is no more, that it closed its doors." He paused a moment. "The songs of your fight with the Kaini are known also. This does not concern us."

"It's true our trading posts are closed," he said. "I have come south to open a new post. The name MacLeod is still respected and I will deal fairly with everyone."

"This is true. Your name demands respect, but be warned. Your post won't be on Osage land. We have too many traders and soldiers already." The Osage paused a moment. "So you should know. I am called Hawk. It's a name you should remember."

"If I live?"

A small smile broke the warrior's stony expression. "You may go, trader. But don't stay long on Osage land. There are many tribes here and much hatred between us. Soon there may be war. If you are captured again, I may let you go free, but others won't."

Sean replied with a wintry grin of his own. "You haven't captured me the first time."

Hawk did not comment as the band of Osage left in a whirl of dirt clods and dirty looks. He breathed a sigh of relief, although his scalp still felt a little loose on his head. Sean couldn't remember why he'd decided to bury the young warrior in this traditional way, but it was a good thing he did. A small thing, but it had turned the tide in his favor.

Hawk came riding back alone. "There is another thing. We look for a young girl, stolen from us a couple of days ago. Do you know of this?"

"I do not," he said. "How is it you speak English so well?"

"These are bad times in our land. If one must know his enemies, he must know what they say."

"Or your friends?" He watched closely for the Indian's response.

Hawk shook his head slowly, turning to leave. "That cannot be."

When Sean spoke in Osage, Hawk's head snapped back around toward him.

"Then go in peace, brother Hawk."

A grudging look from Hawk, an expression of surprise, and the Indian once again walked his horse from the clearing.

The clearing was finally deserted and the only sound was a crow cawing noisily as it looked at the body on the burial stand.

At the back end of the clearing, close to the trees, Buffalo Shield rose from where he'd been lying in the tall grass, holding a lance nearly eight feet long decorated with feathers and scalps. He spoke softly behind him and a piebald horse rose like an apparition, shaking off the grass and leaves sticking to its sides.

The Indian smiled grimly as he leaped on the back of the horse in a single bound.

He'd counted coup by lying with his horse in plain view of the Ghostrider and the Osage warriors. They were within a few feet of him when the warriors examined the track he'd left.

As he gazed down the trail the Ghostrider had taken, he grunted his contempt and rubbed his warhorse between the ears. The horse's skin rippled and jumped, the tail flicking restlessly, but made no sound.

Riding slowly over to the burial platform, the Indian pulled the blanket aside and looked at the young warrior. He didn't know the face, but wasn't surprised. The warriors from his particular band of Bloods were all dead. In a moment of introspection, he wondered if his hatred was getting the young men killed.

When he started his journey, he'd sent young men to watch the trails bordering the great river. Once they spotted MacLeod, it was easy to pick up the trail. He was in no hurry because he left nothing behind. For some reason he couldn't define, he wanted to study his enemy.

Several times during the journey, he'd planned an ambush only to have it foiled at the last minute. When the Ghostrider rode on the wooden boats, he'd been hard put to keep up. He was tiring and so was his pony.

Finally, he caught one of the men after leaving the boat that carried his prey. It only took moments for the man to tell Buffalo Shield all he knew. The Ghostrider was headed to a place called Kawsmouth, where a river called Kansas, or Kaw, flowed into the mighty river he followed. Buffalo Shield turned away from the river and headed south.

He missed him at Kawsmouth, but he caught a Nez Perce who didn't like MacLeod. The brave was not so brave and told him the Ghostrider was going south to the White River country. He made the young warrior beg for his life before he killed him. As a Blackfoot, Buffalo Shield hated Nez Perce more than he hated the Ghostrider. They were old enemies.

Finally, his mind stopped wandering and he looked again at the young brave. He reasoned the young warrior on the platform must have been one of the scouts he'd sent out and the warrior then decided to take care of the Ghostrider on his own.

It had been a long journey from the upper Missouri. Buffalo Shield knew full well the passage of time was dulling his hatred and lust for revenge. When he thought of it, revenge for what? Was he getting old and soft? He shook himself as if to rid his body of the offending thoughts.

He turned the horse away from the burial platform, fingering his medicine bag. His voice was soft in the morning sun filtering through the trees as he chanted.

> I am Buffalo Shield. I am alone.
>
> White traders killed my family. The bodies of my woman and sons lie behind me, buried in a cave high above the trees where only the eagle and wind will see.
>
> I have seen our young men die.
>
> The Ghostrider, MacLeod, came among us. His anger was a burning fire that destroyed our best warriors. As many as I have fingers and toes, he killed. When he left our country, many young warriors followed to avenge their brothers and the honor of our clan. They did not return.
>
> I ride the spirit trail.
>
> Mother Earth gives me life. Father Sun gives me fire. Wakan Tanka will give me death. The spirits give me strength. The bear and panther show me the way. Though I understand his anger, I will follow my people's enemy far to the south to learn his ways. I will eat his food and drink his water until his spirit and mine are one. I will shadow him until he is looking over his shoulder all the day, and bait him until

he begs for an end. Then, I will kill the Ghostrider.

I am a warrior.

My age shows my skill, my bravery is shown by the scars of battle. When I look back upon the land of my fathers, it does not speak to me. There is nothing to keep me from my final journey.

My heart is stone.

I am the last of the Bloods, a warrior clan of my tribe. I will not be lonely. I have my bow made of buffalo horns. My lance has killed the huge bear of the north. My knife and tomahawk are stained with the blood of my enemies. The red sash of the Blood clan hangs from my waist. The spirits of my brothers and my sacred weapons will keep me company.

I shall not return to my father's land.

I have counted coup this day on the white man MacLeod and the Osage called Hawk.

It is enough.

Six

A mule is a perverse beast in the best of times. Given a routine to follow and no chance for mischief, it will normally do twice the work of a horse — but a mule is never normal. For hundreds of miles the pack animals had been up at dawn and traveling on the trail an hour later, all without change in the routine, until this particular day.

Sean didn't like Old Grey and the dislike was mutual. But that was all right, because Old Grey didn't like much of anything.

The mule had been lying in the tall grass most of the morning, waiting for Sean to finish the burial, and then the confrontation with the Osage had added more time to the delay. Trouble was, while the other mules waited patiently, Old Grey liked the comfort of the tall grass. He liked it a lot.

With the usual amount of cursing and yelling, Sean got the mules headed up the trail, but kept looking suspiciously at Old Grey. The mule was about as trustworthy as a porcupine in your bedroll. Still, they were moving right along without much trouble, and even in the right direction.

Even though. . . . He turned in the saddle and searched the forest behind him. For the last two days he'd felt uneasy. Even before the night attack by the young warrior. He had that uneasy feeling that always came when someone was tracking him.

He constantly searched the forest. If someone had a game to play, he wished he knew the rules. He nodded his head, confirming his own thoughts to himself. That was why he had found the tracks. It was intentional. Then a cold feeling came over him. Whoever left those tracks had walked right through his camp without him knowing it. The pure brass and gall of it would be a mighty way of counting coup against an enemy held in contempt.

He sighed and pointed Thunder's nose up the trail once more. They had to make up some time, and the sun was already high above them. Maybe it would be a good day after all.

The land he traveled through had been changing in the recent days. When he picked up the trade goods from Chouteau, he also picked up a map of the rivers south of him. When he left the Missouri River at Kawsmouth, he'd struck south, crossing the Osage River and the Marmaton and then at the Neosho, bearing east to Anderson's Post on the James and south along the White. The flat plains gave way to the rolling foothills of the Ozark Mountains, and it became increasingly hard to find an easy way through.

In the distance rose the first of the mountains, one with the top seared off as if by a giant fiery sword. The Ozarks did not compare in size to the Rockies, what the Indians called the backbone of the earth, but did compare to them in sheer roughness. He relaxed in the saddle as he let Thunder find his way down the faintly marked trail.

A chorus of blood-curdling screams interrupted his thoughts as a band of Indians broke from the cover of a ravine. Thunder stood firm, but the noise stood the mules straight up on their hocks. An arrow buried itself in Old Grey's rump. The terrified mule rolled its eyes and let out a wild bray, drowning out the yipping war cries of the Indians. Old Grey spun on his haunches, made a hard right turn off the trail, and launched straight into the whooping band.

The tether rope, looped tightly around a metal ring sewn on his saddle, snapped tight as a bowstring and shucked Sean and the saddle off Thunder's back, leaving the horse kicking and sunfishing like the mules. He hit the ground still on the saddle, and rode it in a cloud of leaves and dirt behind the bucking and frantic mule.

He briefly saw the other mules bucking like grasshoppers in every direction, braying and snorting, with their packs slung under their bellies and eyes wild in panic. Old Grey plowed through the warriors, took another hard right around a tree, and left for Canada. The rope finally ripped loose from the saddle and the momentum tossed Sean face-first into the base of an oak tree.

He rolled over, spitting dirt and blood, fighting to come up with some kind of weapon. As the dust slowly settled to the ground, he heard the strangest sound. Laughter. From a Cherokee war party.

His head pounding in pain, he tried to sit up and pull his fighting knife, but somewhere between thought and action, he just faded away.

Sean dreamed again, but this time the dream was different. Somewhere deep within him he was grateful. The dream was white-hot, with confusing shapes and sounds. Pain lanced through him, and then the rain came suddenly to cool the heat.

Spluttering and coughing, he opened his eyes to the sun shining brightly through the trees and a Cherokee warrior wearing buckskins and a beaver hat standing over him with an empty water bag. The warrior grinned like a banshee at midnight.

Sean sat up holding his head, groaning as he looked around. Thunder stood close by and was saddled. Several warriors led two of his mules toward them. There was an extra pack on the ground, and a large haunch of meat starting to drip as it hung over a fire.

He pointed at the meat. "Please tell me that's my damned old grey mule."

The Cherokee chuckled. "It is. We prefer mule meat above all other, although that one was stringy and tough."

"Even better than catamount?" He stood, casually looking around and making conversation that sounded stupid, even to him Holding his back with one hand, he rubbed his throbbing head with the other, trying to force the dizziness away. While he rubbed his back, he felt for his belt knife, and looked around for his rifle. "You're welcome to the old hammerhead. You'll probably have to cook him for another week before you can eat him."

He finally searched out his weapons. Seeing them in a pile next to the fire, he edged that way.

The Cherokee held up his hand. "There is no need for your weapons. You are safe enough . . . for now."

Stopping, he looked closely at the Cherokee. The Indian was dressed in a homespun shirt and buckskin leggings. A beaver hat adorned with beads and feathers sat slanted on his head. The knife at his belt was plain and looked very functional. The haft looked worn from use.

He shook his head, and immediately regretted it. The pounding was so bad he hated to move his eyes. "That's the second time today someone's told me how safe I am, and I nearly died both times. You speak English well."

The man shrugged, amusement showing on his face. "My mother is Cherokee and my father is a French trapper."

He weighed his chances of fighting his way out of this and didn't like the odds. "You know, just for a minute there, I thought you were attacking me."

The Cherokee grinned. "We were, until the fun started."

He ruefully rubbed the knot on his forehead. "Some fun. Don't you and your friends have some sort of work to do, like fishing, hunting, or maybe trapping? I mean, other than chasing poor, innocent pilgrims around the forest?"

"Innocent? Now, that's a strange word from the son of a MacLeod. It's even stranger from the feared Ghostrider, the killer of so many Blackfoot warriors. You don't seem to be very poor, either, from what we found in your packs."

He was beginning to think he had a town crier going before him to announce his presence. "Just a figure of speech. I lost whatever innocence I had a long time ago. Did you leave me anything?"

"We took only a few trade items. Some knives and lead for bullets." The Cherokee continued in a serious tone. "It's a bad time to be in these hills. There is much death." He suddenly grinned. "Things to laugh at are hard to find."

"Glad to help." He gazed around the circle of faces. "What's your name?"

"You would know my name to steal my spirit?" The Cherokee's voice was incredulous as he mocked surprise.

He couldn't help himself and laughed. "I think your spirit is safe enough."

"I'm called Red Eagle. If I ever had a white name, I don't remember it."

Grinning, Sean reached out his hand and the Cherokee shook it in the way of the whites. "Sean MacLeod."

"One of our men recognized you. What brings a fur trader from the north to our land?"

"I'm just passing through and maybe looking for a place to settle. How did your man know me?"

"You travel fast, but not as fast as our hunters and scouts. Many of the tribes trade with their northern brothers. No one gossips more than a bunch of men around a campfire. Many people know of your trouble. We know what brings you here and you must know that, whatever land you pass into, a decision must be made whether you are friend or enemy and if you may go or stay."

"It's a strange thing." He rubbed his head. "I've passed through the lands of the Blackfoot, Arapaho, and Sioux. The Otoe, and Fox. I've traded with all of them from time to time. Since I left Kawsmouth and up to now, I've hardly seen a single Indian and not many whites — just when I stopped to trade. Today, I've been attacked by a Blackfoot, threatened by the Osage, and damned near run over by a whole herd of Cherokee. I think my luck's running out."

"I think your medicine must be pretty good, since you're still alive." Red Eagle grunted in disgust. "It's a good thing word of your travel goes before you. Most think you would make a better friend than enemy. But understand this, MacLeod. The whites from the east are pushing all the tribes into this land. Each of our tribes is different, and should not be here. Many old enemies are being shoved together and are unwilling to make peace. I think the white fathers hope we'll all just kill each other."

Sean shook his head. "Well, I wouldn't know a 'white father' if I saw one, and actually hope I never do. As for me, I'm hoping to set up a trading post somewhere. I would be honored to trade with the Cherokee."

"Have you asked Hawk?" the Cherokee asked in a chiding tone. "The Osage claim all this land and refuse to make peace with anyone. War hasn't broken out yet, but the Osage are very unhappy."

His voice hardened. "I had a few words with Hawk. And I'll not be asking anyone's permission."

Red Eagle looked at him for a long moment, the smile gone from his face. "It's good to be brave . . . not so good to be foolish. We'll see which you are."

He thought a moment about the situation. He knew things were bad on the upper Missouri, with the more warlike Blackfoot pushing out the Cree and Nez Perce, but it sounded like he'd traded one problem for another and stepped into a situation that was a powder keg waiting to explode.

"You mentioned many deaths. Who's doing the killing?"

Red Eagle shrugged. "We don't live in big villages like the Osage. With us, there's never more than a few families living together, and scattered all over. Men go out to hunt and don't come back. Other hunters find bodies. Who knows?"

Baffled, Sean asked, "No Osage arrows, moccasin prints, things dropped in a struggle, nothing like that?"

"Nothing." The man spoke bitterly. "But we've found no Osage bodies, and that tells a story."

If it weren't for a twist of fate and one man's sense of humor, he could easily be lying dead next to his mule. If he were a cat, he'd be running out of lives soon. "Thanks, Red Eagle. I owe you."

The Indian shrugged and smiled. "Not really. It was pretty funny."

With a sharp command from Red Eagle,

the band of Cherokee leaped on their horses and plunged back into the dense forest. They left the fire burning and most of Old Grey's sizzling hindquarters went with them. Enough remained for a small meal. The day wasn't all bad. He'd get his revenge on Old Grey. If he could chew him.

Seven

The Cherokee named Running Buffalo paused behind a tree, his gaze on the whitetail deer grazing in the tall grass ahead of him. The sun was close to setting, leaving the forest in a surreal dance of light and shadow.

The deer was easy prey to an experienced hunter, and the Cherokee was almost bored with the process. Every time the deer raised its head to look around, it would telegraph the move by switching its tail. Running Buffalo would simply freeze until the deer lowered its head again. Silently, he eased out from behind the tree, thinking how easy the deer was to kill.

Running Buffalo never saw the man whose arm snaked around his neck, and with a contraction of vice-like muscles, cut off his air. The Cherokee dropped his bow, hands going to his neck, clawing at the arm. So painful was the grip on his throat he almost didn't feel the blade slipping between his ribs. The slight prick of pain in his side turned into white-hot burning. He lurched away in panic and almost pulled free, but the arm held tight around his neck. Running Buffalo's legs scuffled the forest floor in a spasm of misguided energy set off by his oxygen-starved brain. As his sight faded into blackness, he saw the whitetail deer bounding away.

Buffalo Shield knelt beside the dead Cherokee, cleaning his blade on the slain man's buckskins. He looked around the shadowy forest for any sign of other hunters, but there was nothing. Even the birds weren't paying attention, and they were the first line of sentinels in any forest. His thoughts were contemptuous as he looked the man over. He'd died so easily. But then, he was a Cherokee.

Turning away, his thoughts turned inward.

I am Buffalo Shield and the land I ride is strange, and wild. There are many different tribes, all warring against each other and with the whites. Two days ago, I counted coup on the Osage, and today a Cherokee has died under my knife. These men are children who play at war.

Today, I stood in the Ghostrider's tracks and drank from the pool where he slaked his thirst.

I walk his path. Soon, by his actions and his spirit, I will know him. The white man I seek is making friends. People respect him without knowing what he is. This day I saw him laughing with the longhair Cherokee warrior. He will relax soon, and let down his guard. I alone know him. I alone know what he can do. He does not know me.

Sean poured another cup of coffee from the fire-blackened pot. The cup and pot clinked together as he searched the forest around him. The sun peeked over the tops of the hills in the east, casting a grey light in the depths of the trees.

It'd been two days since his ruckus with the Cherokee and Osage. Since then he'd been alone. Packing away the rest of his camping supplies, he was lost in thought a moment. *Maybe that wouldn't be so bad . . . being alone.*

He walked out to the edge of the bluff he'd camped on, looking over the country. Far below, the White River wound its way through the valley. The Indians called it Niuska. Straight across from him on the valley floor, smoke rose lazily from a huge chimney on the back side of the trading post. From the posts he'd seen before, he knew there would be an equally large fireplace in a great room used for cooking and heat.

Looking closely, he could make out a trail winding down the mountain and ending up across from the compound below.

To his left stretched the Boston Mountains, hazed in blue while the rounded tops humped above the fog-shrouded foothills. Off to the west the land flattened out, turning into rolling prairie and grasslands. A beautiful land and one he wouldn't mind staying in.

Later, after Sean started winding his way down the mountain, a lone Indian stepped from the forest, his war pony following like a well-trained dog. He used the butt end of his lance to stir around in the dead coals of the fire pit. With a grunt of satisfaction, he leaned over and picked up a bone from the rabbit cooked the night before. Ceremoniously, he washed the dirt from the bone and meat, squeezing his water skin to make a stream of water. Then, slowly and with satisfaction, he ate the rest of the meat from the bone.

Standing, he tossed the bone back on the pile of ash, his face a stony mask.

As he walked to his war pony, his vow echoed through his mind. *I will drink his water and eat his food, and I will own his soul.*

Having navigated the steep trail off the mountain, Sean walked his horse down the bank toward the shallow river below. His pack mules followed in a shower of dirt and rocks as they slid in behind him. Belly deep in the cold water of the White River, water so cold he had to lift his feet from the stirrups, Thunder hunched his back, his skin rippling from head to tail and then pointed his nose toward the small settlement on the other side.

Jones Mill was a community born of necessity. Some of the swift waters of the river were diverted into a manmade ditch, providing a steady stream to turn the huge paddlewheel of the mill, which in turn was used to grind up grain and saw lumber. The trading post stood next to the mill, and close by to that was a corral attached to a livery stable and large barn. Several log cabins helped form a rough circle and log walls joined the houses together. A few more logs made into walls and they might be able to call the place a fort but it had a long way to go.

As he rode down the middle of the compound, he noticed a building set aside from the others. Several horses stood hitched to a rail in front and men in blue-sashed coats looked at him curiously as they lounged on the porch. One of the soldiers raised a hand in silent greeting, nonchalant and automatic.

Sean rode on by, acknowledging the gesture with a short nod before reining up at the stable. The building was as empty as the corral. After poking around a moment, he glanced back toward the soldiers. They returned his gaze, but made no move to offer comment.

Since there did not seem to be anyone around the building, he unloaded the packs and turned his horse and mules into the corral. Looking into a shadowed corner, he found an old pitchfork with enough unbroken tines to pitch some hay to the animals. He stacked his bundles of trade goods in a vacant corner, throwing a couple of old moth-eaten blankets over the pile.

He stood looking around, a dark scowl on his face as he thought of leaving his packs unprotected. He'd have to chance it since he vowed to sleep in a real bed tonight and needed to buy some supplies. Besides, it wouldn't be easy for anyone to steal the huge packs of goods. After Old Grey's demise — he had to chuckle at that though — the mules needed the rest from carrying the added weight from the third pack.

The office door of the Commandant's office slammed open and Corporal Henning poked his head in.

"A new man just rode in, Captain. I thought you'd want to know." The corporal stood waiting expectantly.

Captain Isaac Frane paused a moment, then dropped the dispatch he'd been studying. The damned Osage were nothing but trouble. He held in his hands the latest word from his superiors at Fort Smith. *Use your own judgment in dealing with the hostiles.* That one word summarized their opinion of the Osage. *Hostile.*

He pushed his chair away from the desk and strode to the window that faced the street. A man was just crossing the compound, going toward the trading post. Now where had he seen that face? The man was taller than most, broad in the shoulder, and walked with an easy grace. His blond hair tied in the back, eyes shaded by a floppy hat, and dressed like a trapper. His clothes appeared a little nicer than most. Probably Indian made. Squaw man? Maybe.

Captain Frane returned to his desk, opened a drawer, and shuffled through another pile of papers, his mind churning.

Finally, it came to him.

MacLeod! Sean MacLeod. He'd seen him in Saint Louis once, when he was delivering a boatload of furs. He remembered now. His father had owned the Northwest Fur Company, although the boy was one of many sons and probably did not look to inherit. It all came flooding back into his memory, how MacLeod had lost his family and carried out a vendetta against the Blackfoot Indians. Most of his peers considered him one of the finest woodsmen and deadliest fighters of their time.

"Corporal."

Henning leaped up and turkey-necked his head around the partly opened door in response.

"Sir?"

"Bring that new man to me, Corporal. I'd like to talk to him." He paused a moment, thinking of MacLeod's reputation and then said, "You'd better take a couple of men with you."

Sean shifted his long rifle to his left hand and used the barrel to push open the door to the trading post. Once inside, a variety of smells accosted his nose and he felt like he'd returned home.

To his left were benches and shelves

stacked high with trade goods and clothing. The musty odor of cured leather, mixed with the smell of oil from the traps hanging on the wall, and cinnamon sticks in the jar on the counter, assailed his senses as nothing else could.

As he took a deep breath, he thought this was his favorite smell — the smell of a trading post. He grew up in one, and wanted nothing better than to open a post of his own.

Behind him, the other half of the building sported a long bar running along one wall, and a few tables on the sawdust-covered floor. A huge mirror hung on the wall behind the bar, fronted by shelves holding jugs and pewter mugs.

But for now, he needed supplies more than a drink. Stepping into the store, he noticed a sign nailed to a post.

One beaver gets 2# of beads, 1 kettle, and 1# of shot or 5# sugar, 1# tobacco, 2 awls, 12 buttons or 20 fishhooks, 20 flints, 8 brass bells
Four beaver gets 1 blanket
Six beaver gets 1 pistol
Twelve beaver gets 1 rifle

A man walked out from behind the counter, extending his hand. He was short and balding, dressed in homespun white shirt and blue trousers tucked into boots. He had an affable way about him, but Sean noticed his eyes were sharp and searching.

"My name is Jones. Nathan Jones."

He shook hands with the storekeeper. You could learn a lot about someone by their hands, and the hand he was shaking was rough and calloused. Obviously, the man did his own work. "Sean MacLeod. I was admiring your sign."

Jones shrugged, smiling at him. "It saves a lot of questions. I don't like to haggle."

"What if your customer can't read?"

The grin got wider. "Well, then I have an opportunity to make a profit."

Passing the man his want-list of supplies, he said, "Just remember, I can read."

"Are you in a hurry for all this?" Jones asked, looking at the list and ignoring his warning.

"Nope. Tomorrow will do."

He pushed through the batwing doors of the entryway separating the store and tavern and navigated his way through the crowd to the bar. Most of the men just glanced at him, and then turned away. They congregated around a greasy-looking man in buckskins standing at the other end of the bar. He guessed strangers were normal around here and their lack of attention was fine with him.

The barkeeper was a solid looking man with a shock of tangled red hair, huge forearms, and a perpetual twinkle in his eye. He also had the scars of a bare-knuckle fighter on his hands. As he came up, he extended one of them to Sean, his voice clearly heard above the din of voices in the room.

"Fry my lights! I saw you once on the upper Missouri while we were shoving a keelboat up the river. I don't know which one you are, but you were with the MacLeods."

Sean shook the man's hand and it was like picking up a hunk of wood. This had to be the hand-shakingest town he had ever seen. "Angus adopted me as a child and named me Sean. He's a good man who treated me as his own. I can't complain how he treated me."

"Aye. I heard he's a hard man, but fair for all of that. I'm Rob Shay, and I try to run this place. What can I do for you?"

Sean's eyebrows rose. "You own this place? And you're working the bar?"

"Truth to tell, I only own half — I'm partners with Jonesy. And I like to keep my hand in things. I enjoy it. So, what will it be?"

Glancing around, he noticed everything looked solidly built and well kept. He envisioned a place like this for himself. "I'd like something to drink and eat, Mister Shay, then a bath and bed. In just that order."

Their conversation was interrupted by boisterous laughter from down the bar, where the huge man held court to a bevy of admirers. As Sean watched, the man turned his way and the smile froze on the dirty face for an instant, and then the man glanced away.

Sean turned back to Rob Shay with a questioning look. "What's all the excitement? Seems like a mighty lot of folks in here for the middle of the day. Is somebody running for office?"

"Naw, though we've had plenty of that going on. Seem like everyone is practicin' to go to congress or set up a local government. Although, that's the last thing we need. The rumor is we'll be a state soon." Shay's voice took a serious note. "Bad doin's here, son. Someone stole a girl a couple days ago, right out of her cabin. They're guessin' Indians, but I don't know for sure." He threw a disgusted look at the gathering. "These are the defenders of the realm trying to figure out what to do about it."

Sean snorted, thinking of what he'd do of some of his kin were stolen. Then he remembered his slain family and replied brusquely, "The 'what to do about it' should have been done two days ago."

"Aye," Shay said, rolling his eyes. "Now you have a firm grasp of their particular problem."

Shay stepped away a moment and then put a flagon of rum in front of Sean, with a mug, bread, and cheese. "Here. Start on this."

The doors to the tavern slapped open with a sharp bang, and Shay rolled his eyes. "Aw, hell."

Sean, holding a knife in one hand and a piece of bread in the other, watched two soldiers approach.

The bookends marched right up to him, and one reached out and grabbed his shoulder. The man stopped suddenly, and released his hold when Sean's knife flicked up under his chin.

"What seems to be the problem?" Sean craned his head around so he could see the chevrons on the soldier's sleeve. "Corporal, is it?"

The corporal stood his ground, trying to

raise his chin above the point of the knife, while the trooper behind him stood with his mouth open as if wondering what to do.

Shay tried to defuse the situation. "MacLeod, if he pees on the floor I ain't cleaning it up."

He applied a little more pressure with the knife. "I'll keep that in mind, Shay. Well, Corporal?"

"The commander sent us to fetch you back to his office." The soldier's voice squeaked and broke.

"Sounds important. And just who is this commander?"

"His name is Captain Frane," the man said, relief showing on his face when the point of the knife moved from his chin.

Sean shook his head. "I thought you said he was a commander. So, just to be straight, what is he a captain of?"

"Why," the man stammered, baffled at Sean's lack of knowledge, "the army, of course."

Shrugging his shoulders, Sean turned his back to them, and buried his knife in the loaf of bread.

"Never heard of him. And if he can't decide if he's a captain or a commander, I don't want to."

The trooper, who, judging by his actions,

would be known locally for making bad decisions, didn't disappoint his peers. With a curse, he swung a meaty fist.

The swing was slow and ponderous and Sean, who had been watching in the mirror, casually slipped the punch and jabbed his pointed fingers into the man's throat, punching his Adam's apple back against his spine.

As the man fell, gasping for breath, Sean turned to the corporal. "You're disturbing my meal."

The soldier backed away, stooping to help the other trooper to his feet. "You ain't heard the last of this. You can't treat the army this way."

"Army? What army? You're a bunch of rag-tag militia playing make-believe soldier."

Rob Shay leaned his elbows on the bar, hands cupping his face, as he watched the two men exit the room.

"Well," he sighed and then shook his head. "They ain't much, but they're all we got protectin' us from the marauding hostiles."

"You get marauded much?" Sean asked as he watched the men crossing the grounds toward the post commandant through the windows.

Shay was serious a moment, although Sean could tell it was hard for him to do.

"Don't remember any, at least in the last couple of years. Osage are always mighty touchy, but things are pretty peaceful here at the mill. We have things the Indians want, and they have things we want. It works out pretty well for all concerned, but don't tell that to the army. They'd be out of a job."

Sean finished a piece of bread and smiled as he raised his mug in salute. "Guess I'll go see what this captain commander wants."

Shay waved at him and gathered up his plate and mug. "Go on. I'll keep this here for you and maybe have some steak cooked up by the time you get back."

Thinking of the turkey, deer meat, and squirrels he'd been living on, Sean asked over his shoulder. "What kind of steak?"

Shay looked hurt. "You particular?"

He laughed as he walked out. He was starting to like this place.

Eight

The sun was low behind his back as Sean crossed the compound, throwing a long shadow on the building he approached. Walking up the steps, he passed by the soldiers congregated there, and stepped into the office of the commandant. He knew that because the sign said so.

As he walked through the door, the whining voice of the corporal faded to a stop. The two soldiers standing before the commandant's desk turned to look at him.

The man behind the desk stood. "You men get out of here."

The two soldiers shuffled out, giving Sean a wide berth.

"You'd be Sean MacLeod?"

Sean looked at the man, searching his memory but coming up blank. "How is it everyone around here seems to know me? You have the advantage of me, sir."

"I'm Captain Isaac Frane."

"I thought you were a Commander." The captain's blank look didn't say much for his sense of humor. As he studied the man, Sean was sure he spent a lot of time polishing his medals, if he had any. He looked like someone who was a lot more enamored with the idea of being a captain, than actually being one. "I thought the army was mostly in Arkansas, and east of the Big Muddy. Why are you so far north?"

The captain shrugged his shoulders. "Missouri will be a state soon. Maybe as soon as next year."

Sean nodded. An aspiring politician. Paper pusher. Figures.

"The War Department thought our presence here would have a calming effect on the hostiles, and give hope to the settlers. And to answer your other question, news travels fast down the rivers."

Frane strolled out from behind his desk as he continued to speak. "Every trapper who comes this way has a story to tell about you, Mister MacLeod."

"More than likely just stories, embellished more with each telling." Sean wished the man would get on with what he wanted. "Stories are always a long way from the truth."

"You're too modest." The captain stood

with his arms behind his back, rocking up on his toes, and seemed to warm to the subject. "As an heir to one of the largest fur companies in the north, all the tribes know and respect you. Then that unfortunate incident with your wife and child." He paused with a sympathetic look on his face. "How many Blackfoot did you kill in retribution?"

"Too many, Captain, and I'm done with that. Now, if that's all?" He turned to leave.

"Wait. I'm presenting this badly, Mister MacLeod. The fact of the matter is I need you. The army needs you."

"What for?" He couldn't think of anything the army would need him for.

"You can help us as a scout, advisor, or whatever. I plan to launch an attack on the main Osage village in retaliation for the abduction of a little girl two days ago. With you leading, we would save a lot of time and effort."

Sean just stared at him a moment, no more shocked than if he'd seen two bears paddling a canoe down the river. "Are you out of your mind?"

The captain stopped strutting and looked at Sean with his mouth open. Finally. . . . "I don't believe. . . ."

"No." Sean shook his head and held his

hand up, not believing his ears. "The answer is no."

"That didn't take too long." Shay was wiping down the bar as Sean walked back into the tavern.

"Wasn't much to talk about." He was about to expound on the stupidity of the army and men in general when he was interrupted.

"Well, he hasn't given up. He's right behind you."

As the captain approached, several of the townsmen joined him. Sean glanced up at the circle of people, wondering why they didn't have something they should be doing.

"Gentlemen," the captain loudly addressed the group. "This is Sean MacLeod. I've been trying to recruit him to help us in our foray against the Osage."

"Foray?" Sean's voice was incredulous. "Foray? You make it sound like an English foxhunt."

A man in buckskins at the end of the bar had been expounding loudly to several people both times Sean was in the tavern. He was large and looked unkempt, like he'd just come in from the trail and couldn't find a stream to bathe in. He and his followers paused in their conversation.

"Besides." Sean inclined his head toward the man in buckskins, standing at the other end of the bar. "I thought you already had a scout."

"Jake Turner?" The captain smiled. "A good man, I suppose."

Turner scowled at him.

Frane noticed. "Actually, he's a very good man. But with your experience, I think you'd serve us much better. We don't have much, but we could pay. Why don't you reconsider?"

"Hey," Turner called from the other end of the bar. "You never offered to pay me."

Sean just shook his head, thinking of the money represented in his letter of credit. "I told you no. I don't need your money and I don't serve any man. I've got goods to sell and more trade goods to buy." He slipped Shay a sly grin. "Then I'll try to put Jones and Shay out of business with my own trading post. I don't have time to go chasing Indians."

One of the townsmen shouted, "Them Osage need to be taught a lesson!"

"Then, why didn't you go for the little girl right away?" He calmly singled the man out. "You should've tried to get her two days ago, instead of looking for courage in a jug of rum. If the Osage did take her, which I doubt they did, she'll be long gone by now."

Several of the men laughed. One of them said, "You think we care about the girl? She's just a half-breed Osage herself. Better off with her own kind. Problem is, they might get the idea they can take a white girl next time. There's a lesson needs to be taught here."

Sean slowly studied the circle of rum-flushed faces and feverish eyes. He was starting to understand a few things.

With barely concealed anger, he spoke softly. "So, no one even tried to get her back?"

Jake Turner had joined the group. "Her mother's out lookin' around and trying to find her." He laughed. "Hell, she's probably on her back in some Osage lodge right now." The man held out his hand. "My name's Turner, by the way. I don't believe we've met."

Sean turned back to the bar, ignoring the man and trying to control his temper. "Talk to me, Shay."

Glancing side to side at the people next to the bar, he said. "The woman they're talking about is Ellen Mackey. She was taken captive a few years ago, and her husband killed. She escaped and came back here to live. After she got back, she had a child. That's the one who's been stolen away."

"How old a child?"

Shay rubbed his chin a moment. "I'd say ten years old. She's a pretty girl, smart as a whip. The Mackeys mostly stay to themselves, and Ellen hunts to supply meat and fish to the post. Does a little trapping. The local folks sure don't mind eating the food she brings in." He shook his head. "Miz Mackey is good people. She doesn't deserve any of this. I tried to stop her from going, but she went out looking anyways. She was frantic to find her little girl."

"Of course she was frantic. Any parent would be." Sean glanced around at the crowd. "And not one of these brave souls helped her. Not even this fine upstanding Army captain?"

The bartender looked guilty. "No one did. Not even me. I'm too old, and these folks . . . well, you see them."

Sean looked around the circle of faces. None would meet his gaze, and they sidled away from the bar. "Yeah, I see them."

Some of the conversation came seeping back to him as they walked away. He heard words like whore, and slut, as the men discussed the Mackey woman.

Jake Turner was the loudest, standing a

few feet away in a crowd of men. "Aw, that Mackey woman probably liked everything she got. If she didn't want to be raped, she wouldn't have been, that's what I say. If she had any pride at all, she'd have killed that whelp when it was born, an' herself the same time. She's just a no-account whore."

Shay said something and grabbed at his arm as he launched himself away from the bar. With a move too fast for the drunken scout to comprehend, he pulled his fighting knife and put it to the big woodsman's throat. With his other hand, he grabbed a handful of the man's balls, lifted, and squeezed.

Turner took the blow with a grunt, then sucked in a breath and let loose a thin scream, lurching up on his tiptoes, more concerned with the clutching hand than the knife at his throat.

"Now, don't you move, Turner, or I'll turn you into a steer."

He stood close, staring into Turner's eyes. His voice was so soft only those men close to them could hear what he said.

"Now, just how is it that you think a woman could keep from being raped? The Osage are big men. I've seen them up close and personal. Most weigh over two hundred pounds and are even bigger than you are.

They live by physical strength and courage.

"This woman you're talking about is what, about a hundred pounds? Maybe a little more, if she's average. If she could stop an Osage warrior from doing whatever they wanted with her, why don't you stop me?" His voice was thick with suppressed fury. "What about it, big man? Why don't you stop me?"

He squeezed harder, and Turner gave another squeal as sweat popped out on his face.

"Please, mister . . . please." His rum-soaked breath came in short little gasps. "I didn't mean nothin'. It's just talk. I'm sorry."

"It's not me you should be apologizing to, mister. It's to the lady and her daughter for being a spineless coward. Talk like that can get you killed."

He became aware of a spreading hush in the room. A bottle clinked on glass, there was a soft muttered curse, and then just the breathing of the men around him. Without relinquishing his hold on Turner, he glanced around toward the door. His breath caught in his throat and he thought for a moment Angie had walked through the door.

The woman stood in the threshold of the entranceway. Dressed in buckskins that were dirty and torn, she had a knife in her waistband and a short-barreled musket held lightly in one hand. Her tangled, dark hair was done up in a bun, with several strands escaping to fall past her shoulders. Her startling blue eyes surveyed the room, her scrutiny coming to rest on him for a moment, then moving on. Almost as if she were surprised by something, her gaze came back to rest on him. She stared at him a long moment and it seemed she almost staggered, and then her gaze finally settled on the Army captain.

She looked dead tired as she leaned her musket against the wall, and then purposefully strode across the room. She walked with a rolling gait that only a woman can do, and every man in the place appreciated it.

For the first time, he noticed she wore the same half-length moccasins he did, and looked approvingly at the haft of another knife nestled in her left boot. As she passed by, the scent of soap and flowers drifted to him. A clean smell, even though her buckskins were dirty and stained.

"Captain Frane, I've come to ask for your help again." Her voice was low and throaty, and slightly hoarse. "It's been two days. I just can't cover enough ground by myself."

"Now, Ellen," the captain held his palms out toward her in a placating motion, "we're all sorry about your daughter, and you know we'd all be out there with you if we thought it would do any good. Those Indians that took her are just plumb gone. Besides, the men here have their own homes and families to think about."

"Isn't your army supposed to be here to protect against things like this?" She gazed around the silent circle of men, shoulders slumping. "I see how it is." Her upper lip curled in disgust. "I'm sorry to have disturbed you . . . *gentlemen* from your work." Her tone of voice left no doubt as to her opinion of the men in the room.

As her shoulders slumped and she turned wearily to leave, all the hope seeped out of her. Sean resisted the urge to reach out to her. Looking beat, she walked past him toward the door.

He must have momentarily relaxed his grip because Jake tried to move away. A squeeze, followed by a twist brought another squeal from the trapper.

A few feet past him and almost to the door, she stopped abruptly, as if she just couldn't help herself, and slowly walked back to him.

"I'm going to hate myself for asking this,

but what are you doing to Turner?" She glanced from the knife down to his hand. "Are you going to kill him, or just play with him? You might not need the knife, you know. He'd probably let you do that anyway."

The surrounding dark hair set off her deep, blue eyes. It was some mix between black and deep brown, and she had a bridge of freckles across her nose. On closer inspection, she could have been Angie's twin. Even the voice was the same. He shook his head, trying to make the image go away.

His hand left Turner's crotch, but not before he gave a final twist. The man slowly sank to the floor with a moan, curling into a ball as he clutched his groin.

Returning his knife to its sheath, he looked into her eyes, trying not to get lost. "Why, nothing like that, ma'am. Not at all. We're just having a discussion about opportunity."

They both stepped quickly away as Jake Turner gave up several meals and a day's worth of rum in a retching cough.

She stared frankly back at him, and a spark erupted within him that he thought he'd never feel again. Their eyes locked together a few seconds past proper, before she looked from him to Turner, and back again. Her left eyebrow slowly rose to an arch. Without speaking a word, she retrieved her musket, walked through the doors of the tavern and on into the store.

Knowing her troubles were none of his business, he still followed her. He was being drawn into something and wasn't sure if he should struggle or not. He thought of what Walker had told him about the spider's web and the fly.

As he walked into the store, he heard her speaking to the owner. "Nathan, I'll have to buy on credit. I don't need very much."

"You're credit is always good with me, Ellen." His tone was deferential and it was easy to tell that Jones liked and respected her.

Stopping behind her, he said, "Ma'am, if you'll excuse me. I've heard some talk of your troubles. If the Osage truly have your daughter, you're going about this the wrong way. They'll probably try and sell her to the French. You can probably buy her back. I'm pretty sure they won't harm her."

She looked at him a moment, then replied in an exasperated tone. "Mister, I don't know you or anything about you. But I just heard 'probably' twice, and then a 'pretty sure'. It must be a real comfort to have such firm conviction of your opinion." Her anger built, and her eyes welled up with tears. He wanted nothing more than to take her into his arms. "You don't know they won't harm her. You don't even know who has her. Even now. . . ." She caught herself a moment and used her last amount of strength to shore up her courage. "Besides, I have no money for ransom, Mister . . . ?"

Jones interjected, "Ellen, this is Sean MacLeod. He's a trader from up north, and probably knows more about Indians than anyone I ever heard of, from Canada down to the Gulf of Mexico."

Sean gave Jones an exasperated look as her expression brightened momentarily, and he could guess what was running through her mind. She was wondering how to get him to help, what to offer, and the best way to do it. As she was about to speak, he interrupted her.

"Missus Mackey, I just can't. I'm looking for a place to settle and start a post of my own. I just don't have time."

He looked at her and knew how bad that sounded. For some reason it tore at his heart to say it, and wished he hadn't. "Ma'am, I truly wish I could do something."

Her shoulders slumped in defeat. "It's all right, Mister MacLeod. I'm used to it. You should fit right in with the rest of the men around here. I hope you find what you're looking for."

Not able to let it go, he watched as she turned back to her food supplies, ignoring the accusing glance from Jones.

"They'll not harm her."

She whirled around angrily, shouting into his face. "You don't know that. You have no idea what it's like to be captured by Indians, of what they can do."

"All right, I don't think they'll harm her," he repeated stubbornly. "She's just a young girl."

"Not that young. In a year or so, she'll be old enough for them to. . . ." Violently shaking her head, he felt her tears splatter on his face.

"Look, either they'll sell her, or one of the women of the clan will adopt her. It's just the way they do."

"Go peddle your ideas somewhere else, MacLeod." Her voice was cold, brittle, and soft at the same time. "I don't need your help . . . or your advice. I have to find my daughter. She can't be left with them, or raised by them." Her eyes welled up in tears again. "Whoever in hell they are."

He was still watching her and feeling guilty as she left the building. Turning to Jones, he said plaintively, "Well, they won't!"

Jones shook his head. "I guess that depends on a lot of things, now don't it?"

Nine

Buffalo Shield sat cross-legged before a small fire. Naked except for a loincloth and buffalo horn headdress, the myriad scars on his body covered him like a blanket — badges of pain and fury, and a lifetime of glorious battle.

He slowly fanned an eagle feather through the smoke wafting upwards from the glowing coals as he chanted softly. It would soon be dawn and his spirit would come back to him, invigorated from roaming in the night. Finally, the sun rose to start a new day. His thoughts rose with it.

I am Buffalo Shield and I have touched the Ghostrider. Soon, I will own his spirit. Soon, he will die.

Sean jerked awake, sitting in a bed of tangled, sweat soaked sheets, and feeling as if he had run all night.

The dream was new, full of haunting images and hatred. The Indians would call it a spirit dream. The whites would call it a crazy nightmare. As he wiped his forehead with a corner of the sheet, he didn't know what to call it. He just knew he didn't want to do it again.

In his dream, he'd been standing alone in a ravine with a huge bull buffalo charging straight at him. Angry. Mean eyes and wild mane, frothing and snorting, crashing through trees in his fury to trample him. The ravine was narrow and the walls seemed to be closing in. Barely, he'd dodged out of its way and was still fighting and running when he woke up.

His pounding heart settled into a steady cadence, along with wistful thoughts of a restful night's sleep. He rose, dressed, and went to stand by the lone window in the room. It was still dark, but dawn wasn't far away. The sleeping rooms were in the second story of the trading post, and from downstairs came the first rumblings of people talking, pots and pans rattling, and the smell of food cooking. He studied the small room he was in. It was lucky he didn't have to share it with other travelers, and was convinced he'd have been more comfortable on the ground or in the stable.

Later, after he put away enough steak and

eggs to last a week, he walked out on the porch of the trading post. He put his hands at the small of his back and stretched, groaning as he tried to get the kinks out. He was sure of it now. The stable would've been better.

As he turned to reenter the trading post, he realized he'd made a decision while he slept. It didn't make much sense, but he knew better than to fight it. *Hell, what else can I do?* With a sigh, he accepted the inevitable. He'd go after the girl. But deep down, he suspected the real reason lay in the fathomless blue eyes of the girl's mother. And he didn't understand that either. He thought of Angie every night and most every day, and picked at her death and his guilt like the scab of an old wound.

Shay met him at the counter, handing him a pack of supplies, including an extra powder horn and shot. "You're probably in a hurry," he said gruffly, but with a twinkle in his eye.

"What's this?" Sean's voice was early-morning grumpy, and sandy dry. "Where's Jones?"

"Nathan likes to read late at night so he doesn't get up this early. I fill in until he gets here. Since you're going after that girl, you'll need a few things."

He gave the saloon owner a baleful glance. "When did you decide this?"

Shay smiled. "Just as soon as you walked in the door yesterday. Your folks are good people. You're a good man. Hell, you can't help yourself."

Sean abruptly changed the subject. "Last night in the tavern, I saw someone leaving just as I came in. I couldn't put a name to the face until this morning. Do you know a man named Santee?"

"Yeah, and he's poison mean. He cut up a man or two, and we ran him off. He still sneaks in for a drink, now and again."

Nodding, Sean said, "That sounds like the man I know. Old Angus ran him out of the North Country, along with his partner. He always ran with a man named Charbonneau."

"Is he some kin to them up at Kawsmouth?" Shay scratched his head, a puzzled frown painted across his face.

"No. That's Francois Chouteau running that post."

Shaking his head, Shay said, "All those French names sound the same to me. Why are you interested in him? There are more renegades runnin' around here than you can shake a stick at. One or two more can't make a difference."

"Charbonneau was run out of the country because he was a slaver. He sold captives to the French in Canada. Let's look at your maps, Shay. I need to get the lay of the land."

"You think he could be here, doing the same thing?"

Sean thought a moment. "Well, he's here and I don't think he's seen the errors of his ways. A skunk can't change its stripes. So, yes. I think it's a possibility. Plus, the French are in New Orleans, and the Big Muddy is just a short distance away."

The two men had a map unrolled on a table when Captain Frane stomped into the store. It was a beautifully drawn map, etched into the soft, cured hide of a fawn.

The captain didn't waste time. "MacLeod, you're going with us against that Osage village."

Sean just glanced at him. "Not likely."

Storm clouds built on the captain's face. "Now, listen to me. We are going after those Osage and you are going with us. That, Mister MacLeod, is a direct order from the United States Army. If you don't comply, I'll put you in irons, lock you up, and throw away the key." Frane stood erect, looking satisfied with the sound of his parade ground speech.

Sean glanced up from the map and replied in a calm voice. "Captain Frane, according to this map, the trail to the Osage camp leads straight east along the White River. A child could find it. If you're so intent on committing suicide, I suggest you get on down the trail. You're wasting daylight and my time."

"MacLeod, I intend to get that little girl —"

"Let me get this straight," Sean interrupted in a soft voice, hoarse with barely restrained anger. "You intend to march your soldiers, all ten or fifteen of them that I've seen, and your handpicked drunken townsmen down the middle of a marked trail in broad daylight, take a village of Osage Indians by complete surprise, rescue a girl that you don't even know is there, and return here in time to knock down a few rounds of rum before supper. Is that about right?"

Rob Shay's eyes bulged, and his face turned bright red. Little bleating sounds squeezed from under his fingers, clamped over his mouth.

"Captain." Sean shook his head sadly. "You won't get past the dogs."

As the captain angrily stomped from the building, Sean turned to Shay, who was busy wiping tears from his eyes with a red bandana.

"He looked upset."

Minutes later, Sean rolled up the map. "Shay, how long will it be before the captain can hit the trail?"

"Well, it's a little past daylight. I'd say a couple of hours, if they leave at all. Most of his Indian fighters are still sleeping off last night's drunk."

Sean stood, looking in the direction of the trail, already thinking of the problems ahead. "You'll take care of my animals and packs? If I don't make it back, just sell them and give the money to the woman . . . after your cut, of course."

"Sure, I can do that, but I'd just as soon not go down that road."

"And there's something else to think about." He handed the man the pouch containing the letter of credit from Francois Chouteau. "When this is over, I might be in the market for a post, if either of you are ready to retire."

Shay's eyes got big as he looked at the document. "I'll think about it." He pointed at the pack he'd given Sean earlier. "There's pemmican trail mix and some trade goods in there. Figured you'd be traveling light.

How do you plan to do this?"

"Well, I don't know for sure. The more I think about it, I might just go with a direct approach and ask. If the Osage have her, I might be able to buy her back. If Captain Frane goes stumbling in there with his band of merry men, they'll likely move her somewhere else or kill her." He paused, and then sighed, shaking his head. "I'm just shootin' in the dark. It beats the hell out of me how to do this. All I know is something has to be done right now. It may be too late already."

Shay thought for a moment. "There's one more thing. You best remember these Osage are touchy. Religious as all get out and honor is a big thing with them. Get up and say their prayers every morning. They don't do a lot of trading with us, so we don't know them like we would the Cherokee or Kickapoo. If you spook them, there's no tellin' which way they'll jump."

He nodded. "One other thing to think about and it's about as much a shot in the dark as finding the girl with the Osage."

"What's on your mind?"

He spread out the map one more time. "I came from Kawsmouth and down the old Indian Trace. I figured to follow it on down the Three Forks, and Fort Gibson on the Arkansas. If someone was to need to move some captives quickly, where would he go?"

Shay glanced sharply at him, and studied the map a moment. "Only place I see would be down the White River to the Black, then to the Arkansas. They'd need some flatboats, but there's plenty around to buy."

"And just where does the Arkansas empty into?"

Shay thought for a moment, looking puzzled, and then grinned. "Why, right smack dab into the big Mississippi herself."

"And right down to French New Orleans."

Shay shook his head, tracing the route on the map with his finger. "You have a sinister mind, Mister MacLeod."

He was trying to think ahead without knowing the lay of the land. "Are there any settlements along the White?"

"Well, there's Coker's, and M'Gary's, Matney's, several of them. They're all mills and tradin' posts. Why? What's rattlin' around in that noggin of yours?"

"I can't really put my finger on it. It's just a gut feeling, especially after I saw Santee. Why don't you send a runner that way, just for a heads-up? Who knows, someone might see something. If they do, we need to know it. Tell them I'll pay for a good horse if they have to kill it getting here. In the meantime, I'll go play with the Osage."

"Well, you better treat them like a pet porcupine. Just don't pet them against the grain."

He picked up his rifle and carried his pack out to Thunder. When Shay followed him out of the building, he paused. "What about the Mackey woman?"

"Ellen Mackey? Good woman. Don't you believe any of that you heard at the bar last night. She's tough as nails, too. Not many would have survived around here all alone, taking care of a child, and no man to help. And, there's one other thing that might be the most important." Shay grinned at him. "She can be just a might stubborn."

He thought about it a moment, then sighed. "We're joking about this, but we both know what can happen. I only know one way, and that's to go in swinging and see what shakes out. Leave the latch out, Shay. And keep a bucket of water handy. I may be coming back with my tail on fire."

Ten

The trail heading east along the White was little more than a footpath skirting the river. It was amazing that Frane, who supposedly knew the country, wanted to attack the Osage camp coming down this trail. The best they could do would be two or three abreast. The Osage children and their dogs could cut the patrol to pieces before they ever got to the main camp.

According to Shay's map, the Osage village lay where the next creek, named Bull, fed into the White River. Not far as the crow flies, but a good three hours along the path.

Once away from the settlement, Sean pushed his horse into a steady trot, slow up the steep hills and making speed where he could. Most of the trail was in canopied shadow, with the sun barely up. Fog still rose in places off the water where cold springs fed the river from below. Huge hardwood trees draped over the trail, making a canopy that would be cool in the summer heat.

Within the first few minutes he came upon signs of a bear where a rotting log lay torn apart in search of grubs. Then there was the flash of a white tail as a deer bounded away into the gloom of the forest, late for a day of rest after a night of feeding. Everything he saw convinced him this was a good country to settle in.

Rounding a bend in the trail, he encountered a vision. With her long, black hair highlighted by a shaft of sunlight, Ellen Mackey sat on a deadfall by the trail. She was a beautiful woman, even though as he got closer he could see her blue eyes were red-rimmed from crying and fatigue. It was his thought she'd dressed for him, as much as she could. Her hair was combed and fell to her shoulders. She'd changed from buckskins to homespun and her blouse was tight and didn't leave much to the imagination. Knowing she didn't like him, she must have been really desperate to try this.

Sean pulled up a few feet from her, steam rising from the Palouse in the cool morning. His thoughts went immediately to Angie and how she used to look.

She calmly returned his gaze, not saying anything.

"You wouldn't have had a sister would you? Her family was wiped out? French? Name of Delavault?"

"What on earth are you babbling about?" From her expression, he must have grown two heads. *Well, hell.*

"You just look like someone I used to know. Pretty women shouldn't be alone out here."

"Only pretty women?" Her left eyebrow rose as she looked at him. Her spirit showed through her pain and exhaustion, saucy and pert. His mouth was dry, just looking at her.

He sighed. "I was just trying to throw out a compliment. Forget I said anything. So, what do you want, Missus Mackey? What do you want from me?"

"That's easy. I want to help you find my daughter. You will need help, and I know the country."

Although he thought he knew the answer, he just had to ask. "How did you know I'd be coming this way?"

"Rob Shay is a good friend. He said you'd be along as soon as your brain woke up. To be honest, I'd about given up on you."

He thought a minute, taking in her brick-red shirt worn over homespun pants. It hurt him to see her beauty marred by gauntness. Her face was a conflicted study. While her eyes showed a spirit he'd rarely seen in anyone, man or woman, her face was smudged with dirt. A small welt rose on her cheek that probably came from a small tree branch whipping her as she passed by. She looked strong and tired at the same time.

With a sigh, he dismounted and dropped the reins to the ground, knowing Thunder wouldn't move. He figured they had a little time to spare. He took off his hat and wiped his forehead.

"Can you keep up?" he gently asked her. "Your horse looks more worn out than you do."

"She's my daughter, Mister MacLeod. I'll keep up, because I have to. If the horse drops, I'll run. But I'll keep up."

"What manner of weapons do you have? Or do you plan to spit in their eyes?"

She lifted a musket. "Not as fine as your long rifle, but more serviceable in the close woods, and I have knives in my pack."

"Better you should save your pack for food. That musket has poor range and less accuracy. Maybe you should go on back to the settlement and let me handle this."

Lifting the musket suddenly, she pointed it at him. "I pack this with a double load of powder, and then put whatever I can find down the front." She turned an innocent face to him. "It is the front that things come out of, isn't it? Mostly I load it with nails and pieces of metal from the blacksmith shop. Run straight away, left, or right. If I pull this little thing on the bottom, I think someone called it a trigger, you'll be dead before you reach the trees."

Inwardly he was smiling, but he carefully reached out and gently pushed the barrel away with his finger. He belatedly remembered she'd been bringing in meat for the settlement for years. "Let's not be pointing that thing my way. I'll take your word for it. If you accidentally bump the trigger, that blunder-buss will take saint and sinner alike."

She gave him a level stare. "Then, I won't hear anymore nonsense about my not going with you?"

"I don't suppose I can stop you. It's your life. I might as well have you where I can see you as running around where I can't. We'll see what we can do about getting your little girl back."

"Fine." She got up from the log, and put her hair into a ponytail. She slapped on a short brimmed hat. "Let's get to it."

As he turned to his horse, he thought he heard, "Beth."

"What?" he asked.

"Her name is Beth. She'll be ten years old tomorrow, and is very likely scared to death."

"Short for Elizabeth?"

At her nod, he smiled as he turned away. "If she's half as tough as you, likely we'll find her chasing a bunch of Osage down the trail with a switch."

An hour down the trail, Sean stopped to give the horses a breather in deep shade from the towering oaks surrounding them. The land fell away from one side of the trail, and rose to the top of the peak on the other. Overlooking the valley, vultures circled looking close enough to touch, although they were hundreds of feet off the ground below.

"What do you think?"

"Vultures, and a lot of them." He was painfully aware of how close she stood. He hadn't been with a woman since Willow at Kawsmouth.

She made an exasperated sound. "I can see that. Shouldn't we go see what they are so interested in?"

"It would cost us an extra hour, and a hard trail getting there." He paused, thinking of all the different things that would bring out that many of the carrion birds. One likely cause he didn't want to think about. "It could be a deer."

"We'll not know if we don't look, now will we?"

"Don't get snippy with me."

"I'm sorry. It's just that . . . for that many birds to be in one place, it could. . . ." She paused a moment. "I would think with your history, you could understand my feelings."

He looked at her a moment, then simply nodded and began negotiating a way down the mountain.

They spent the better part of an hour traversing the mountainside. Finally, they came out at a dimly defined trail, dotted with sunshine where the dense shade let it through. Letting the horses take a breather, he sat gazing at her.

"What?" She looked at him oddly. "Why are you staring at me?"

"Oh, there's a lot of reasons for me to stare at you. You're a beautiful woman, and easy to look at. But I just wondered if you want me to go ahead by myself."

"Because . . . ?"

"What if it's your daughter?"

Her gaze remained steady. "Then I'd want to know, wouldn't I? You can't put off pain just because it hurts. You should know that."

"Sometimes the Indian isn't too kind to prisoners," he said, thinking of his own loss.

"It might be better to not see."

"Mister MacLeod," she said firmly, "I won't fold up at the first sign of trouble."

"Fine." He resigned himself to losing another verbal battle. Was she always this obstinate? "Let's get to it."

Another half hour passed before they came to a small clearing, hearing the beating of wings and raucous mutterings from the carrion birds. When she started to go forward, he held out his hand, stopping her.

"We'll wait."

As they sat their horses, well back from the edge of the clearing, Ellen watched a change came over MacLeod. She was startled and fascinated at the same time. His voice had turned so quiet she had to strain to hear, and that quietness affected his whole body. As if a veil dropped over his face, or a curtain on a new play, she suddenly saw the man who generated the stories she'd heard, the man who had killed scores of people in retribution for the deaths of his wife and son, and as the stories went, never from ambush. Always giving the other man his chance, he gave them honor, even in death.

Watching him, she was suddenly afraid . . . she didn't know this man, was unsure of him, and she valued her quick judgments of men. Even more frightening was the attraction drawing her like a moth to a flame. It caused her to be cross with him when she didn't mean to be.

"Is something wrong?" she asked in a soft whisper as she looked around them.

He didn't answer, gaze intent as he studied the clearing and surrounding trees. Finally he moved his fighting knife to a more comfortable position, and then clucking gently to his horse, slowly eased into the clearing. She brought her mount up beside his.

To one side, partially under a bush, was a splash of color. As they neared the spot of bright cloth, a torn dress of red and yellow, they discovered what they both were afraid to find. A young girl lay in the tall grass, with shiny black hair, and a ruddy skin color gone pale in death. The face of the girl was miraculously spared from the abuse the rest of her body had taken from predators. The birds usually went for the eyes first.

"Thank God." Her sense of relief was like a physical blow. If she hadn't been sitting on a horse, she might have fallen.

"It might have been better if it was her."

"Why on earth would you say that?" She whipped her head around to look at him, anger pushing away her feeling of lightheadedness.

She watched as he continued to scan the forest around them. "If it were your daughter, you'd take her home, mourn her, and this would all be over for you."

"Well, it's not over. Not until I find her." She looked at him. "Or have you already decided to quit?"

He did not answer her, just sat on his horse looking at the girl. Finally. . . .

"Odd, don't you think?"

"What do you mean?" She was still upset about his comment, but his calm manner piqued her interest.

"Osage warriors rousted me in camp. They were looking for a girl who disappeared and I'm afraid this is her. You're looking for your daughter. I talked to some Cherokee, and they mentioned a girl missing. They blamed the Osage. The Osage blame the whites. And here we find a young girl, where none should be, and used quite badly. I wonder who will get the blame for this."

She nodded, knowing all too well what he meant. "What are you thinking?"

"I haven't settled on anything yet. Just a thought I can't quite put my finger on. Thinking aloud, I guess. What is that mark on her forehead?"

"She's Osage. That's a spider tattoo, one of their signs of royalty."

"The Osage wouldn't kill one their own, now would they? That leaves us, or the Cherokee. Or maybe someone else we don't know of yet."

He dismounted and pulled a blanket out of his pack. "We'd better take her home."

She gasped. "Are you crazy? You want to take a dead Osage child into her village?"

"Sure. Better we do that, than to have them find our trail and track us down. I'm thinkin' they wouldn't give us time for long-winded explanations. We've left sign here, lady. Besides, we wanted to talk to the Osage anyway, didn't we?"

Looking at him, she shook her head as she dismounted to help wrap the girl in a blanket.

"Lord, help us."

Eleven

They'd been traveling barely an hour when an Osage sentry stepped from behind a tree. Although the Indian was armed, he didn't appear particularly hostile. Sean was puzzled about that until he caught movement in the trees on both sides of the trail. The man didn't need to worry. He had plenty of help.

"Take me to Hawk." He hoped Hawk was from this village.

Without a word the man turned on his heel, gesturing for them to follow. Another surprise. They were expected. Watched. And suddenly it made sense. He smiled and nodded as they walked. The Osage had already found the girl. They'd been waiting to see who showed up. He turned and said as much to Ellen and noticed she was pale, but holding her head up high. She looked proud, and searching a little deeper, he saw she had the good sense to be afraid. Good girl.

Riding into the village with the body of the young girl draped across the front of his horse and wrapped in a blanket, he noted how neat and clean everything was. He estimated forty lodges stood on either side of the main path, with a longer building in the center made of poles and reeds woven together. Women and children lined the sides of the trail, and at the center lodge, the warriors waited. A soft keening sound welled up from some of the women at the sight of the dead girl. He had a moment's thought about Shay telling him the Osage didn't allow strangers to see their women. *Curious.* Maybe it was just other Indian tribes. Or, maybe they weren't expected to leave.

Ellen kneed her horse up beside him. "We should dismount. To remain mounted while they aren't is a sign of disrespect."

His quick thought went back to his own camp. The warriors hadn't dismounted. Apparently, the showing of respect wasn't always given.

With a quick and grateful glance at her, he dismounted and then turned to help her down, although she didn't need it. He could feel her trembling as he helped her, and felt guilty for bringing her, even though she insisted.

"Thanks for the advice, Missus Mackey. I'd forgotten you were held captive here. Are you all right?"

"Well as I can be. And, it was in a smaller village. Not here. Please, I need you to stay close to me. I can't appear weak. I will not give them that."

Turning, he led the small procession of guards they'd picked up toward the warriors waiting at the lodge. She walked beside him, not behind and he liked that.

At a sharp gasp from her, he turned. "What?"

She nodded her head toward one and of the warriors. "He's the one who had me captive, years ago. I thought . . . I hoped he was dead."

He looked over. The squint-eyed Osage with a chip on his shoulder. Might have known.

Hawk stepped forward and raised his hand, stopping them. He was dressed like all the other warriors, with nothing to distinguish him as a leader. "What brings the whites to this village?"

Sean suppressed a smile. Hawk knew damned well what had brought them. Playing along, he replied in a formal tone. "I've brought your small one home after we found her in the forest. And we also helped lead your warriors home as well, although they were very shy and remained in the trees."

"You knew it was a trap?" Hawk asked, surprised.

"Actually, no. I figured it out later. But to admit half your camp has been following me without my knowing it . . . that's a bitter pill to take."

"I have seen better woodsmen," Hawk admitted with a small smile. "I hope there is something you do better."

Almost as one, they turned toward the small bundle tied to Sean's horse. When he turned, he found Ellen right next to his shoulder. She'd taken her hat off and shaken her pony tail loose. Her luxurious black hair fell to her waist. Her expression was defiant, but she trembled as his hand found her arm. Was she was putting on a show for her captors? He couldn't blame her.

Two warriors stepped forward to take the body, and then carried her toward one of the lodges. The keening and wailing started again, as the family began to mourn their daughter.

"I warned you about staying too long in

Osage country."

Before Sean could reply to Hawk, there was a nearby shout. Striding from the crowd of warriors, the narrow-eyed trouble hunter reached for Ellen.

As the Indian grasped for her, Sean's fighting knife rang as he pulled it from its metal sheath. A blade against his throat brought the Indian up abruptly. The edge was so sharp just the touch on the man's skin left a blood trail. The warriors surrounding them surged forward.

She stood calmly, as if showing everyone her man would take care of the situation.

"Hawk, we are guests in your camp and came in peace to bring your small one home. Acting like this is a dishonor to you. Do you wish this man to live?" Sean calmly smiled as he met the gaze of the Indian under the point of his knife.

The chief let the silence draw out a few moments before he answered. "Never-Sleeps is a good fighter. This is a time of much trouble. I need all my warriors."

He increased the pressure of the blade, causing the man to rise on his tiptoes, blood dripping from the point of the knife. The Indian's eyes glared hatred at him.

He repeated. "This man begs for death. If I should kill him?"

"Think what you do, MacLeod."

"If I kill him?" Sean persisted. "This man has shown disrespect to me and to my woman."

"I cannot speak for your safety."

"Then control your men. Or are you not the chief in this village?" He released the pressure on the blade and shoved the man away from him into the arms of his followers.

Never-Sleeps spoke for the first time. His truculent voice was loud as he attempted to save face. "I will kill you, trader. I will kill you, and take this woman again. She-who-was-once-mine and carried my child will warm my bed again this night. It has been many seasons, but I still remember her."

"That won't happen," Sean said, looking at him. "And the child couldn't have been yours. I've heard you are a gelding acting as a bull. Who, among all these great warriors, did you bring into your lodge to breed your captive woman?"

Two men held the struggling Indian as Sean turned back to Hawk, casually sheathing his knife, feeling Ellen standing next to him like a second skin.

"Hawk." Sean spoke softly, as he watched several warriors pull the troublemaker away. "Hear me on this. That man has caused this woman to suffer. It won't be tolerated anymore." He took a deep breath. "A question for you. You have said the Osage know everything that happens in their domain. Who roams these hills? Missus Mackey's daughter is gone. The Osage girl was a captive until she died. I saw the rope marks on her arms. The Cherokee speak of girls stolen from their lodges. Who is out there? Who is doing this?"

Hawk turned on his heel and walked away.

Sean called after him. "Put away your hatred. We can help each other. The white men are blaming the Osage. The Cherokee blame the Osage. Who does the Osage blame for this? The whites? The Cherokee? Do you think either would do such a thing?"

"You are free to go," Hawk said over his shoulder, ignoring Sean's comments. "Do not come to this village again."

"Did the greatest warriors in the land find no tracks? No sign at all? Everything leaves some sign. Who took this girl, Hawk?"

The Osage warrior stopped. His troubled gaze took in Sean and Ellen. His reply was abrupt. "No sign. Now, leave this place before your head is put on a pole in front of my lodge."

"That's twice you've threatened me. I don't like it. Now, here is a puzzle for you. I don't hide well. My enemies can always find me. You found me. The Cherokee found me. Hell, I'm the easiest man to find anywhere." He paused a moment. "I'm still alive."

Hawk looked at him a long moment, and then continued to walk away.

Sean and Ellen exchanged glances as they turned to go.

"Sorry," he said to her. "That didn't go as well as I expected. I thought they might help, or know something. But at least we know the Osage don't have Beth."

Never-Sleeps appeared again with a group of warriors and interrupted Ellen's answer. "I will take her now, white man." His voice was loud and carried across the village. "She will be my woman. She will warm my blankets and have my children. I will part her legs —" His voice ended abruptly with a sound like an ax hitting wood.

After a moment of stunned silence, Osage warriors, shouting threats and working themselves into a killing rage, immediately surrounded Sean and Ellen.

Sean pulled his blade.

"Hold." Hawk came striding back through the village toward them. He barely glanced at Never-Sleeps, whose head was pinned to a pine tree by the broad-headed blade of Sean's hatchet.

"It seems there is something you can do better, after all." Hawk's voice was neutral and controlled.

"It is a curse of mine."

They both turned and watched as the weight of the body finally pulled the blade of the hatchet loose from the tree, sliding wetly down the trunk to the ground.

"Never-Sleeps challenged this man for his woman and lost. This is the end of it," Hawk told to his warriors. Then, to Sean and Ellen, "I tire of warning you. You may go. Do not come back."

He inclined his head toward Hawk, and then turned to go, retrieving his ax on the way. He said abruptly, "Ever hear of a Frenchman named Charbonneau?"

Hawk stared stonily at him, and then turned away.

Sean and Ellen walked past the edge of the compound, leading their mounts, passing a gauntlet of hostile faces and menacing gestures. Stopping past the last sentry, they mounted their horses.

She looked at him with an expression he couldn't read. "You killed that man, like . . . like you'd step on a bug. He was just making empty threats. I've never seen anything so callous."

"Are you defending that polecat? If you

are, then you're on your own, and can go back to the Osage right now. And those weren't empty threats." He stopped and looked at her, wondering what she was thinking. "Did you want to go back? Was it that good for you? Did you like what he was saying?"

She looked away for a moment. "God, no. I hate him for what he did to me. You can't know how much. It just seemed like a senseless killing."

"Well, I'm sorry if I offended your finer sensibilities. As for me, I just didn't want him dogging our trail. It was kill him now, or sometime later. And later might prove disastrous for us. I just figured it would be one less problem for us if he were gone. In the future, I'll try to not hurt your feelings."

Her answer was sarcastic and he sensed her girding up for an argument. "So, I guess I should thank you for killing that man?"

He just shook his head in exasperation. "It would seem appropriate. Next time I'll know better. I'm sure you could have handled that man all by yourself."

Her answer was cut short by an Osage scout, heading for their camp.

"I guess there won't be a surprise attack from the army." Ellen quipped as she watched the man run by them, casting a startled glance their way.

"You mean Captain Commander Frane and his army? They're about as sneaky as a cannon ball." Sean snickered and they walked their horses back down the trail.

"The captain isn't so bad. He's just doing his job."

He stared at her with his mouth open. He could distinctly remember the contempt she'd shown the captain the night before. His eyes narrowed. What the hell? "So, am I missing something here? First, I mistakenly kill the father of your child. Now, I seem to be stepping between you and the captain commander? I need to stop and figure out the lay of the land."

She glanced at him, shaking her head. "You've only been here a day, so you shouldn't judge people so quickly. Captain Frane is a dangerous man in his own right, and he has seasoned troops at his beck and call. They just have to walk a fine line here, since Missouri isn't a state yet."

"Oh, I'm sure they're killers, one and all. I'm starting to understand a few things, now. Why is he not here instead of me? If he's as good as you say, there's no need for me to be here. I could have slept in and then had a big breakfast of Shay's mystery meat and buzzard eggs."

When she didn't answer, and wouldn't look at him, he just snorted. "I don't like being used, Missus Mackey. Even by a woman as pretty as you." His voice was grim as he wondered again what he was doing here. "You know? I'll bet those crack troops of your good captain have been sober just long enough to wonder what in hell they're doing out here, and might be looking for an excuse to go home. Let's go see if we can round them up. Your captain may want to see good men killed, but I don't want that on my conscience."

Twelve

Buffalo Shield stood near the place the Ghostrider found the Osage girl. He was surprised the Osage warriors hadn't killed the Ghostrider out of hand, and had actually let him into their camp. As he watched, he'd seen the Osage shadowing the woman and the Ghostrider. But the larger mystery was still here. Who had killed the little girl? His thoughts were on his own slain family, knowing how he would feel in the same circumstance.

The Osage warriors were children in the forest and had trampled much sign. Curiosity took over and he circled, searching the ground. It took him an hour to find it. A ghost of a trail, hardly even an indentation in the ground. Buffalo Shield stood a moment in indecision. The mystery of the situation finally got the best of him. The Ghostrider could wait his turn at death. He turned and followed the trail.

Sean heard them long before the Army and its ragtag militia rounded the bend in the trail that skirted the river. He and Ellen sat their horses across the narrow trail as the cavalcade ground to a halt in front of them.

Captain Frane was the first to speak. "Ellen. What are you doing out here with this man? It's not proper. You should go back to the post and let us handle this."

"So, you think it's proper to let me run around the countryside looking for Beth by myself? I'll decide what is proper for me, not you or the army."

Sean watched her with his mouth open again. This woman switched trails more often than a blind buffalo.

"I'd have to agree with her, Captain." Her gaze snapped around to stare daggers at him. He smiled at her, really starting to like irritating this woman. "She's much safer with me."

She started to yell at him. "I'll have you know —"

The captain interceded. "Get out of the way, MacLeod. We have army business to attend to. You don't have any part of it." Captain Frane was resplendent in his tailored uniform, every button polished and buckles buffed.

Sean just shook his head. "They don't have her, Captain. Never did."

"How do you know that?" one of the townsmen shouted. "Who else would steal a girl?"

"That's a question you should have asked a couple days ago." He switched his attention back to the captain. "We didn't get off to a very good start yesterday, Captain Frane. We're not doing much better today. Maybe that is as much my fault as yours. You told these folks earlier that I know my way around Indians. If you believe that, take my advice and turn around. Nothing can be gained by your attack on the Osage."

"These hostiles need to be taught a lesson."

"What lesson would that be? They're only hostile if provoked. It's plain stupid to walk up and knock down a hornet's nest if you don't have anywhere to run. Would you teach them how to survive when the whites are pushing all the different tribes into this one little area? Or how to feed their families when the animals they use for meat are run off by so many people?"

Frane stood in his stirrups, trying to stare him down. "I have my orders, Mister MacLeod."

"Yeah, I'll just bet you do." He decided to change his approach. "Where did you learn tactics, Captain?"

"What the hell? That is none of your business."

"Well, if you're so good on strategy think about it. You've got about thirty men here, including your soldiers. Missus Mackey and I just left their village. I counted over a hundred warriors in that camp behind us. They are all first class fighting men. They're not a bunch of hung-over drunks and misfits. It's no secret the Osage warriors are feared by every tribe who has ever met them. Don't you wonder why? There is a reason for it. They love to fight and live to fight. An Osage woman won't take a man as her husband until he's killed an enemy. I'm betting there are a lot of single warriors in that camp looking for a wife. You'll be killed in no more time than it takes them to boil their favorite dog for lunch."

The captain shifted uncomfortably in his saddle. "We'll catch them in their village and surround them. With surprise on our side, we should prevail." His voice faded away.

Sean shook his head, looking at the forest around them. He finally looked at the captain. "Do you actually think they're still in their village? My God, man. They knew you were coming a half hour ago. They could hear you." He looked pointedly at the greasy trapper behind the captain. "They could probably smell your scout. How are you sitting your horse, Turner? Not too sore, I hope?" Turning back to the captain, he continued. "Unless I miss my guess, we're surrounded right now."

Frane tried to argue. "We have to keep order between the tribes. Something has to be done."

"You're correct. But not today. Find another way."

One by one, the men at the back of the raiding party turned back toward the post, leaving the captain and his soldiers alone on the trail.

After watching some of the men leave, Captain Frane stared at him angrily. "This isn't over, MacLeod. You've undermined my authority and I won't forget it. I'll see you back at the post."

"At your pleasure, Captain. But don't make this about you and me. This is about finding Missus Mackey's daughter, or did you forget that?"

The captain angrily pulled his horse's head around and made back toward the post.

As the small cavalcade of soldiers followed the captain toward Jones Mill, a lone Osage warrior walked out on the trail and stood looking after them. He was too far away to be sure, but Sean thought he saw a disappointed look on the Indian's face as he faded back into the forest.

Sean turned his horse toward a ghost of a trail that led into the hills and away from the river.

"Where are we going now?" Ellen hurried to catch up.

"Oh, you're going with me, now? I thought you'd go with your toy soldier."

"Very funny, MacLeod. I'm just glad you didn't kill *him.*" She pulled her horse alongside. "All the men around me seem to wind up dead or injured if you're around."

He just shook his head. *Blind buffalo.* "We'll go back to the starting point, where we found the body of the Osage girl. We can camp the night there, and then see if we can pick up any sign in the morning."

"The Osage didn't find anything, so why do you think we can?"

"Well, now. Maybe they didn't. Maybe they did. All I know is I don't trust Hawk any farther than I can throw his horse. There may be something there for us to find."

"I've been over most of this part of the country in the last two days, but it was just a once-over. There just wasn't time." Her voice trailed away.

"We'll find the girl, or find where she lies. That's a promise."

"Beth. I told you, her name is Beth."

"Are you always so obstinate?" Then he looked at her, seeing the hurt and anguish. "Sorry, my mistake. We'll find Beth, wherever she is. However long it takes. I promise, and I don't take promises lightly."

She turned her head away, but not before he saw tears glistening her eyes and heard her faint sounding voice. "Thank you. I mean that."

They found a place to camp in a natural grotto closed in on three sides by limestone walls. A cold spring welled up from under a huge boulder, surrounded by fern and grass cropped short by grazing deer. Sean cleared a spot under a twisted cedar at the edge of the clearing, and made a small fire surrounded by stones. The tight foliage of the cedar would dissipate any smoke, making it hard to see from a distance. Not that the local Indians didn't know where they were camped, it was the whites he worried about.

Knowing Ellen was in no mood to talk, he

quietly went about the business of fixing something to eat. The stores Rob Shay had sent along — mostly beef jerky and hardtack — did not appeal to him, so he'd unpacked his longbow and dropped a small doe earlier. Doing the small tasks around the camp gave him time to think . . . and he had a lot of thinking to do.

To survive long on the frontier, the one thing you cannot believe in is coincidence. Animals don't change their habits. Deer will walk the same path to water every time, use the same trails to go from one feeding place to another. You can catch a catamount in the same trap as its mate, simply because the bait is there, and it's in their nature to try to get it. You can't get within a mile of an antelope on the prairie because they are too skittish. But tie a piece of red cloth on a stick so it blows in the wind, and they will walk right up to it . . . and your gun. It's simply in their nature.

Thinking along those lines, he remembered as he'd walked into the front door of Jones Mill he'd seen a man named Santee slinking out another door of the tavern. Santee ran with a slaver named Charbonneau. *Some girls are missing.*

He stood looking into the hills. "It's their

nature," he said to himself. "It's just gotta be."

"What?"

He jumped slightly. Ellen had sidled up behind him on feet quiet as any mouse.

"I'm just thinking aloud. It's a habit acquired when you're much alone." And he'd been alone too long.

She stood quietly beside him, and he liked her for it. She didn't break the mood of the evening with idle chatter. He liked that too.

Chewing a salty piece of venison, she finally said, "You know? You'll make someone a fine wife someday. I could get used to this. How about it? You stay home and raise the kids, and I'll hunt for us."

He smiled at her. "Hardtack and deer meat would get old after a while. But thanks for the offer."

She stood quietly a moment, relaxed in the evening twilight while he watched her.

"Can't you find something more interesting to watch?" Her voice was soft.

"Not likely. I've already seen trees and bushes, and they are nowhere near as pretty as you."

She gave a very unladylike snort. "What about the Osage up on the ridge trying not to be noticed?"

"He can get his own girl . . . and he's a

Cherokee." He laughed at the absurdity of the situation. "The Osage are watching us because they just naturally hate whites. The Cherokee are watching because they are out of ideas about the missing girls and want to see if we come up with any. We're leading a damn parade around the forest and it's a wonder they don't stumble all over each other."

She looked sideways at him, and he noticed she did not argue with his premise. "What did you mean 'gotta be'? You've got an idea what's going on, don't you?"

He took a deep breath, gathering his thoughts to explain to her. Maybe talking about it would help nail down his theory. "I can't prove it, but here's what I think. There was a group of trappers up north led by a Frenchman named Baptiste Charbonneau. Thing is, he was run out of that country for slaving. Mostly he bought young girls, captives and such, from the Indians, and sold them to the French. He wasn't above stealin' a lass or two on his own. That's how I met my wife, Angie. He'd bought her from some Indians who'd killed her family. She got away from him at our post."

Her reply was indignant. "You've seen this man here?"

"Nope. I doubt I'd see him without his

trying to kill me. Who I did see was his runnin' mate, a man named Santee. I saw him leaving Shay's tavern."

"And your thinking is?"

He looked into those cool blue eyes and said, "I'm thinkin' a big group of men will be a hell of a lot easier to find than one little girl. I'm thinkin' everyone is looking in all the wrong places." After a moment, he continued. "We also need more supplies. Guess we might as well head back to the post in the morning."

He expected an argument on that. When she didn't answer, he turned to look at her. When he caught her expression, he glanced around. "What?"

"Do you know that Indian?" she asked in a tense voice.

"What Indian?" He replied. "The Cherokee? Or the Osage that have been spying on us all along?"

"MacLeod, you need a keeper," she said with disgust. Pointing up an adjoining trail, she asked, "Who is that?"

He saw an Indian leading a magnificent stallion toward them. As he watched, the man mounted his horse in a single leap, holding a spear in one hand and ax in the other. His hands never touched the horse.

Sean's voice turned hard. "Get behind

me. Right now."

She gasped, and then moved behind him and a little to the side as she got a better look at the Indian.

"Missus Mackey, what you see coming toward us is an honest-to-God Blackfoot warrior of the Blood clan. He's straight out of the worst nightmare you've ever had. Right now, he's coming peaceful, so maybe . . . just maybe he wants to talk. Don't trust him. All that hair you see on his lance is the real thing. He'll kill us both without a moment's thought. Don't ever forget that. If it comes to a fight, you hustle back to the post. Don't stop to watch."

He mounted his horse and kneed him forward to meet the new threat. And threat it was. He knew it, and by the tenseness of the horse under him, Thunder knew it. Most people who lived in towns on the frontier would tell you there's no way of telling between a peaceful Indian and a wild one. They are wrong. Now, the Osage and Cherokee were tough men in battle, but you could reason with them on occasion. What Sean saw in front of him gave him the same reaction as when he'd once walked around a boulder and came face to face with a grizzly.

Even the warrior's piebald horse had war

paint, with red circles on its flanks and black circles around the eyes. Eagle feathers adorned the mane, but the halter was braided leather, tough and secure. The warrior dwarfed the horse, and though an older man, he rode straight as the spear he held in his right hand. A buffalo hide shield hung from the side of the horse and what looked like a buffalo horn headdress hung over the shield. The man's waist held a red sash and fighting knife. In the brave's other hand was a ceremonial pipe ax adorned with bloody hair, and the more useful hatchet hung at his waist.

When he heard a sharp intake of breath, he knew she hadn't followed his advice. He wasn't sure whether to be angry or proud. She had put herself in danger needlessly. But, on the other hand, she had his rifle with the business end pointing right at the warrior.

Ellen's voice was soft. "Is that a . . . ?"

". . . fresh scalp," Sean finished for her. "He's been a busy boy."

Thirteen

Sean stared at the man in the early evening light. The smaller horse the man rode stomped in the dust of the trail, ears flattened while it snorted and bared its teeth. If it was trying to intimidate Thunder, it was a waste of time. The Palouse was doing his best imitation of going to sleep.

A breeze picked up and the scalp fastened to the spear swayed slightly. He imagined he could still see drops of blood on the skin side of the trophy. The taking of hair wasn't common in the North Country and he wondered where the Indian had picked up the habit. Both the French and English used to pay bounty for scalps, but soon found out they couldn't tell if the scalps came from friend or foe. Most stopped paying the bounty when they figured out they were buying their own people's hair.

His thoughts went to the warning he'd got at Kawsmouth about a great warrior and medicine man coming to end the journey of the Spirit Trail.

The huge Indian, sitting straight on his horse, put a lot of effort into looking unconcerned. Sean wasn't fooled, and if anything it made him more alert. This man had come for a reason, and the reason was to add another scalp to his collection. Without being too obvious, he scanned the surrounding area to see if the man was alone.

It was quiet, so quiet he could hear Ellen breathing behind him. She smelled of flowers and he wondered how she did that. Even in this tense situation, she woke a longing in him that threatened to break into his concentration.

Finally, he got tired of the impasse and ended the staring contest between them. "The Siksika warrior is far from his home." His use of the generic term for the Blackfoot would get a response from the man. His pride would let him do no less.

"I am Buffalo Shield and I am Kaini, what you call Bloods," the man said in a deep, baritone voice, as if the mere mention of his name answered all questions. "And you are the Ghostrider."

"My brother from the north knows me. And, you should. You've been following me long enough." At the mention of the name Sean was called in Blackfoot country, all pretense of a friendly visit vanished. He desperately wanted to dry his sweaty palms and his mouth was dry. Instead, he settled his breathing and calmed himself, knowing this could get ugly in a hurry.

Buffalo Shield spoke again. "You killed many of my people. Many lodges mourn because of you. Your spirit is strong. I have come to see your spirit flow with your blood onto my knife."

Ellen gasped behind him, but ignored her. "We all mourn. Your people killed my wife and son. I have killed men in battle. Has not Buffalo Shield killed many in battle?"

"As many as have come to me."

"It's been a time of death for both of us. Now we must decide on death or life. I have no quarrel with you. We are not enemies, you and I, unless we choose to be."

When the Indian didn't answer, Sean made sure his tomahawk was loose in his belt. "Buffalo Shield has a message? Would you share the fire and food in my camp?"

The Indian stared at Sean a moment and for the first time the Indian was unsure about something. "What is it that you do here, that the Osage let you go in peace?

Are you allied with the Osage? Blood brothers?"

He realized the Indian warrior was as curious as the antelope watching the cloth fluttering in the breeze. "I am not. Their path is not mine. We look for a young child, the daughter of Ellen Mackey." He indicated the woman behind him. "Also, other girls were taken from their homes. The Cherokee, Osage, and this woman have all lost children."

At the mention of her name, Ellen stepped forward. "Do you know anything of this?"

The Indian barely glanced at her. "Buffalo Shield does not steal children."

Sean turned his head and spit on the ground between them. His voice was hoarse. "Maybe not, but you can sure as hell kill them." He felt himself trembling and knew the old hatred and anger was getting ready to explode. Images of laying his slain family in the grave played in his mind and his breathing quickened. The old anger boiled up and he was powerless to stop it. His grip tightened on the haft of the fighting knife at his side.

Ellen placed her hand on his leg and gripped him hard. Even in this setting, it was an intimate gesture and the surprise of it calmed him. He glanced down at her, read the concern in her expression, and marginally relaxed. But trust in a Blackfoot was not going to happen. Not this day.

The warrior stared at him a moment, his own anger apparent in his eyes, and Sean thought the fight was coming. The warrior was ready. He was ready. It was time to end this.

He decided to wait him out. Ellen was less patient. "Well? Do you know anything about this?"

Buffalo Shield finally addressed Sean, ignoring her. "My family died at the hand of white traders. The traders were not of your clan, so you would not know of this. My heart is empty. There is nothing left for me in the land of my fathers. It came to me in a Spirit Dream that I must have purpose. I must do something, to live or die in honor. My path became clear. The Ghostrider killed many of my brothers. For this, I have followed you from our homeland. The spirit trail the young men rode to their death will be over when I kill you. I must avenge the young men. There must be blood."

Buffalo Shield paused, waiting for Sean to speak. When he didn't, the Indian continued. "Thinking on this, I believe there is also honor in helping you. I would help you find these girls, and those who take them. It will be a remembered battle and a great coup." He looked at Sean a moment. "White men are strange to me. Your thoughts travel a different trail. Do you intend to kill them?"

Ellen spoke up before Sean could. "You're talking of a truce between you and MacLeod?"

"For this one purpose." He looked at Sean. "For now."

Sean took off his hat and wiped his forehead across his sleeve. "Would you two mind if I talk a little here?"

Ellen smiled at him, and shrugged.

"For your information, Buffalo Shield, you and I are more alike than you think. And, to answer your question . . . yes I will kill them. When we find the men who have taken the girls, we won't spare them. We made a mistake not killing these men in the North Country. If we had, none of this would be happening. But what makes you think we need help finding these girls? I already have a good idea of who might have taken them. All I need to figure out is where they are hiding."

Buffalo Shield looked his disdain at Sean. "It is known the Ghostrider never tried to hide his trail from those who would follow. I have been in your camp, and left a footprint to let you know of it. I hid in your camp when you talked to the Osage. None of you saw me."

"Why didn't you join your brother and attack me, then. Why wait?"

"Do not hurry your death, Ghostrider. When it is time, I will find you. While you were wandering, lost in the forest, I have found the trail missed by you and the Osage."

"Where?" Ellen asked. "Where is my daughter?"

"From the place the Osage girl was killed, I followed the trail up this mountain behind me. I lost it, for now." Buffalo Shield shrugged. "But I will find it again."

Sean gave a short laugh. "From what I've seen, whoever this person is should be called the ghost. If it is Charbonneau, he may be a match for the mighty Buffalo Shield in the forest."

The Indian mulled the information over. "I do not know this name."

"He is the slave trader who was run out of the North Country before I left. I'm told he likes young girls, especially Indian girls. They are said to bring more money."

"Why did you not kill him then?"

Sean shrugged. "My father, Angus MacLeod, is a peace-loving man. He stayed my hand and let them go. Ellen and I will return to the post for supplies. We may be on this journey a long time. Buffalo Shield, if you would stay and scout the trails, I'd appreciate it. Help us find this man and where he is holding the girls."

Buffalo Shield didn't look happy, but finally nodded.

Sean continued. "We'll meet you here in two days."

"Two days?" Ellen interjected. "No. We should find the trail now. We can't wait two more days. My daughter —"

Buffalo Shield interrupted her and spoke to Sean. "Your woman speaks much and hurts my ears. I will help, for now. But do not forget. When this small spirit trail is over, we will fight, Ghostrider. There must be blood. You cannot avoid this."

"You have a short memory. Didn't you say that I never hide my trail? Have you ever heard of me avoiding a fight? I would wait for your braves in the open fields . . . you know this. Unless the warriors come at night, like the last young warrior, and he had his chance." He paused. "No, I won't run from the great Buffalo Shield. I'll sharpen my knife for you. As you say, it will be a much remembered fight. There will be blood."

Ellen watched, big eyed, as the two men

stared at each other. Finally, she said, "How about we find the girls before you two start cuttin' each other up? Unless I miss my guess, you'll get a belly full of fighting before this is over."

The man gave them both a look of derision, shook his head, then turned his warhorse and rode loose-jointed like a sack of potatoes back up the trail and into the trees.

The shadows were long and a whippoorwill sang in the distance when Sean took the saddles off the horses and led them to a grassy spot, staking them far enough apart that they wouldn't get their tethers tangled in the night. Since Buffalo Shield had interrupted his meal, he strode back to where his fry pan heated over a hatful of fire surrounded by stones.

He was surprised when Ellen threw some venison in the pan to cook, and once it sizzled, dropped in a few hardtack biscuits to soak in the grease and warm up. His old, beat up coffee pot simmered on one edge of the fire. Once the venison was cooked, they both cut off pieces and ate right out of the pan. He washed the meal down with coffee.

He spoke politely, knowing she was as close to erupting as the hot grease in the pan. "Ellen, would you mind cutting off another piece of meat and fixing that?"

She looked at him like he was crazy. "You're still hungry?"

"Nope."

Standing, he strode to the edge of the firelight and called out. "Red Eagle. You might as well come in for some hot grub before you roll in your blankets tonight."

In a couple of minutes, a horse slowly approached the camp. "I'm coming in."

Sean returned to the fire and sat on a log next to Ellen. She refused to budge, so they sat closely melded against each other.

Red Eagle strode into the firelight and sat on the other log they'd dragged up for a seat. He pulled a hunting knife and speared a biscuit. "How did you know?"

"It was kind of hard to miss your silhouette wearing that beaver hat." Sean grinned at him. "Ellen, this is Red Eagle and a good man. He was kind enough to cook one of my mules awhile back."

She looked between the two men.

Red Eagle just shrugged. "Not much of it was edible. Even the wolves couldn't eat it and the buzzards flew on by. We went through a few days later and the meat was still there."

"How goes your search?" Sean asked, wondering if they'd made any progress. He couldn't believe with all the Indians living in this area no sign had been found of the girls.

Red Eagle shrugged again and continued eating. Finally, he finished and wiped his mouth on the sleeve of his buckskins. As he stood, he said, "Thanks for the grub."

Sean called to him. "Red Eagle, we're going back to the post. We'll meet a Blackfoot tracker here in two days. He claims to have found a trail. Then we'll go after the girls."

The Indian paused. "I saw that Blackfoot and thought you were gonna be dead. That's a mean man yonder. You think the girls are still alive?"

"I'd almost guarantee it." He recounted his theory about the slavers. "You can't sell a dead captive, and I think that's what this is all about."

The Indian seemed to think about it, and then he spoke. "Two days. We'll be around if you need help."

"One more thing," Sean said. "That old Blackfoot warrior you saw who's sneaking around the woods? Try and stay clear of him, because he's poison."

"I know. We believe he's already taken one of our men. If we catch him, you'll need a new tracker." Red Eagle nodded once at them and then, leading his horse, walked into the night.

Sean was surprised Ellen didn't move once the Indian was gone. They sat enjoying the night sounds until the fire was just a pile of orange coals.

Finally, she spoke softly. "I don't know if I have a sister."

Puzzled, he glanced at her. "What?"

"You asked me once if I had a sister, and I don't know. I was raised in an orphanage and boarding school in Saint Louis. It was a Catholic school and very strict. The headmistress was determined to turn out highly educated girls for marriage to suitable businessmen." She paused to look at him. "I hated it."

He smiled. He couldn't imagine this woman being herded around by a bunch of nuns. "So what happened?"

She shook her head and laughed softly. "I was always making trouble. One day, after my sixteenth birthday, they called me into the office. A man was there and I could tell he was either a trader or trapper by the way he was dressed. The headmistress said the man needed a wife, and while she didn't say it, I'm sure they wanted me gone. He didn't look so bad. At least he was shaved and clean. I was desperate to get out of there, so I said yes. Money changed hands and the deal was done. One of the friars had a small ceremony and I walked out a married woman." She looked at him until he held her gaze. "There was no love between us, but he was a good man who treated me well."

"How did you happen to be captured?"

"Oh, that was easy. At least, it was easy for the Osage. I said my husband was a good man. He was also very trusting. We were coming up the trail next to the White River, much as you must have, when a band of Osage jumped us. My husband didn't even have his gun out. In a shorter time than it takes to tell the tale, I was a captive of Never-Sleeps. I'd heard stories of captives but never dreamed the reality of it. Never have I worked so hard or been used so much. I bided my time for two months of the worst Hell I could ever imagine before I escaped. Luckily, we were close to the White River and I followed it north and ran into Jones Mill. Rob Shay and his wife helped me and gave me work."

"It must have been terrible." He couldn't imagine what it would have been like for a naïve girl fresh out of boarding school.

"It was. By the time they captured me, I was no innocent. After all, I was married. But I'd never imagined . . ." She paused a moment. "I had the support of the community until the baby came. Then, except for a few people, it was as if I had cholera. I was tainted and dirty. Since there was no place to go, I stuck it out."

She shivered and he put a blanket around her shoulders.

Looking seriously at him, she said. "You know, there are implications with what you just did."

"Not really." He couldn't understand why his hands were shaking. "That would take agreement by both of us, and we haven't agreed on anything. Anyway, you were chilled and I gave you a blanket. I wouldn't presume anything else."

"You say I look like your wife who was killed. Maybe fate is taking a hand." Ellen smiled at him. "Wait until you see Beth. You won't believe how much she looks just like me. She's out there. I can feel her. All we have to do is find her."

She was still staring at him when he stood. "Like I promised. We'll find her." When it looked like she was about to say something else, he interrupted. "I'll sleep closer to the horses. You can stay by the fire to keep warm. I'll see you in the morning."

Sean and Ellen rode into Jones Mill in

strained silence that lasted the entire three-hour trip back to the post. She hadn't changed her mind and wanted to continue on the trail and saw no sense in coming back for supplies. Only when he threatened to leave her did she relent. After seeing the Osage up close, and Buffalo Shield, her fear of capture was palpable, and he didn't blame her. He couldn't imagine the courage it took for her to search the forests before he came, with no help from anyone.

She finally broke her silence. "We don't know what is happening with Beth. She could be . . . they . . . dammit, we're wasting time."

He was trying to be patient. "Missus Mackey —"

"Don't you think it is about time you called me Ellen?"

He thought about it. He wasn't sure he could. By being formal, he could keep her at arm's length. If she ever got inside that barrier that he had set up, he wasn't sure he could handle it.

"I don't know if I can. That would imply that I like you. So far, you've been nothing but a pain in my backside and I'm tempted to sell you to the first trapper I see."

She just smiled at him as if she didn't believe a word he said. Hell, he didn't believe it either. He shook his head. *Dammit.*

They pulled up in front of the store. "It's still a stupid idea." She continued with little pause. "We are wasting time, MacLeod. I don't like it a bit."

"You said that already. And call me Sean. The way you say my last name, it sounds like a curse. After all, we did spend the night together."

She turned a skeptical eye on him. "I'll try. But, it just doesn't fit you. Besides, you weren't very forceful last night. You might have brought me around to your side."

"Or took your knife in my belly. We've only known each other two days."

She looked at him seriously. Her gaze never left his eyes. "How long does it take?"

He started to answer, but closed his mouth. How long did it take? The sound of footsteps stomping on the porch stopped any answer he had.

"Well, I see you two are gettin' along just fine," Rob Shay said, as he came out of the building. "You two make quite a pair. Pretty soon you'll be thinking of marriage."

Ellen had apparently seen and heard too much for the day. She gathered up the reins of her horse, mounted, and they could hear her voice trailing behind her. "Of all the. . .”

Sean and Shay looked at each other as she pounded down the street away from them.

“Now, what was all that about?” Shay stood, absentmindedly rubbing his head.

Sean watched her leave with a worried frown. The last thing he needed on the trail was someone as flighty as Old Grey used to be. There would be enough trouble. They’d talked long into the night about her situation. He felt her only focus was on getting her daughter back. With all that’d gone on, the two days they’d known each other seemed like weeks. Had he missed her signals? He shook his head. Maybe he needed her to be like Willow and take matters in hand, so to speak.

Shay chuckled at him. “You sure have a way with women. I’d think that, since you two spent the night together, she’d be more impressed with you.”

Sean glared at him, but couldn’t argue with the logic.

Fourteen

Beth Mackey opened her eyes and stared at the canopy of leaves above her. Today she would be free . . . or dead. She carefully looked around in the early morning darkness that comes just before the sun paints the tops of the trees on the mountains. The smell of evergreens in the clear, cool air combined with the scent of cooking meat over a fire and coffee boiling in a pot. She lay listening for any sound from the camp. All was quiet except for the lone guard sitting on a log by a freshly stoked fire and the gentle snoring of the girl sleeping close to her. Easing her legs to a better position, she contemplated the ropes binding her ankles, and the caked blood staining them. Today was her tenth birthday, and she had made a decision to act.

She'd been a captive four days. Her mother had to be looking for her, because all she knew was hard work and doing things for herself. The townspeople would be no help and never had been as long as she could remember. And she knew what they thought of her. Her mother could pass for Indian, except for her blue eyes. For herself, the heritage of her Osage father ensured she was bigger than most girls her age, with raven wing hair and dusky coloring, enough so that the people of the settlement treated her as if she didn't belong. Her mother gave her the will and determination to survive. And smarts, lots of smarts.

Looking around, she tried to count the captives, but could not be sure of a number. Men had come and gone yesterday, sometimes bringing in girls, and sometimes taking one away only to bring them back later. One taken away hadn't returned. She feared for the girl's life, because she'd looked sick, and wobbled on her feet as they led her away. The one man she knew to stay away from was a Frenchman called Charbonneau, who stared at her a lot. Just the look of him made her sick with fear. He'd spoken to her once, asking where her folks came from and if they'd ever been to Canada. She knew of Canada from her mother trying to see to her schooling, but that was it. The man had finally walked away, shaking his head. It was as if he knew her.

She had given up trying to talk the other girls into escaping. Most were simply too afraid to try. Their time was running out. The talk around camp was that they would move very soon, maybe today. Any hope of rescue would be lost once they moved. She had to help herself, and soon. It was up to her to make something happen.

The men would release the girls so they could eat breakfast, but they would watch them very closely. But a call to nature? Now, there was a possibility. Usually they were taken as a group, but if she were alone? She lay quietly, watching the camp come slowly to life.

A few more cooking fires rekindled as men rolled from under blankets, scratching and cursing, staring at the hills around them. The longer they stayed in camp, the more the men became disgruntled and apprehensive — in a word, dangerous. She'd heard them talk about it being only a matter of time before the Osage or Cherokee found them. Finally, one of the buckskin-clad men came up the little knoll where she and a few other girls had slept.

She tried to struggle to her feet, but tripped on the hobbles tying her ankles together. As she awkwardly pitched forward, the man grabbed her by her hair to keep her from falling.

"Ouch! Keep your hands off me, dammit."

The man just grinned and pulled her around to face him. "Watch your mouth, little thing." A muttered curse in Cherokee linking his lineage to a dog came from behind him. He whirled toward the other girl, a slim young woman in a beaded buckskin skirt and black hair in braids. "You shut up."

Trying to deflect the man's attention away from the other girl, Beth stood teetering as she said, "Mister, I need to go to the bushes. I'm about to bust."

The man thought about it a minute while she wondered just how slow his mind was. "You have to wait for the group. Those are the rules."

She tried to look seductively at him, though she had no idea how to do that. She knew she was big for her age, but not that big. But it was all she had. "Can't you take me by myself? Just this once?"

The man leered at her. "Now that can be arranged, if that's what you really want."

She looked at him with big eyes and replied with a soft voice. "Oh, it's what I want."

The man's sudden enthusiasm scared her

and she wondered about her decision. If she couldn't break free, would she go from the frying pan into the fire?

"Boy, you Indian girls learn early, don't ya?"

"So, take off these ropes." She smiled at him. "I can't do it all tied up."

The Cherokee girl looked at her, raising her eyebrows, and Beth shook her head slightly. The last thing she needed was company. Or disapproval.

The burly and foul-smelling man knelt and unfastened the ropes binding her feet together, and then stood. She held out her hands, hoping he would untie her wrists.

He shook his head, glancing down at the rest of the camp. "Now that just ain't going to happen, Missy. I can't chance that."

Giving him a small smile, she held out her wrists again. "It will be better for us."

Staring at her, he relented and started to loosen her hands when one of the trappers in the camp below yelled and pointed toward the forest. Someone ran toward the camp, and the men gathered around him. With a curse, her captor rushed back down the hill, grabbing up his rifle on the way.

She didn't hesitate. She turned and bolted into the forest. As soon as she did someone shouted. They wouldn't be far behind her.

She risked a glance behind and saw the man coming back up the hill. The Cherokee girl threw herself at the man's legs.

Not knowing her exact location, she only knew she needed to go downhill toward the river. The first chance she got, she worked her way down the mountainside, running where she could, sliding and holding on to small trees to slow her descent on the steepest parts of the slope.

She stopped a moment to catch her breath, listening to the sounds of pursuit behind her. It sounded like one man, and he was gaining on her. She couldn't outrun the man, so she looked for a place to hide. The area around her was wild and strewn with huge limestone boulders choked with underbrush and small trees.

As she stepped around a rock as big as a cabin, a brown arm snaked out and jerked her off her feet and into the shadows. She tried to scream but strong arms held her firmly against a body hard as iron, and a huge hand covered her mouth. It was obvious the man was Indian by the forest smell — and just as evident he was not a white man by the stealth he had used to capture her. Slowly she relaxed. Once she did, the man lowered her to her feet. When she looked at him, he held his finger to his lips in the universal sign to be quiet.

A man came down the slope, creating a small avalanche of leaves and dirt. The huge warrior left the shadows and went around the rock. The running sounds ended with a sound like a startled bleat of a lamb, then a solid thump of an ax striking something hard. Then the forest was silent, except for the distant sounds of the men in camp yelling at each other. She hoped other girls had taken the opportunity and escaped.

The Indian came back around the boulder and Beth, seeing him clearly for the first time, almost ran again. He appeared to be old, but had a youthful spring in his step. His body was bare to the waist and scars covered his chest and shoulders. She had never seen anyone dressed like him, and her gaze drew to the bloody scalp he held.

She spoke to him in Osage, and then in Cherokee. She couldn't stop looking at the blood dripping from the hair in his hand. "What tribe are you? Where are you from?"

He surprised her by speaking in English. "The small one is all right? Unharmed?"

Before she could answer, there was a shout from above and a bullet ricocheted off the limestone boulder next to them. The warrior whistled sharply and a horse appeared out of the trees. Throwing her unceremoniously onto its back, he leaped up behind her and spun the horse away from the pursuit.

"My home is that way." She pointed the opposite way they were going. "Please take me home."

"So are your enemies. First we get away, then we get you home."

Home. He said home. She turned and looked into his face for a moment, unable to believe what he'd said. "Do you mean it? You'll take me home?"

"White men lie. I do not. I have made a promise."

She couldn't let that remark pass. "Well, I just happen to know a lot of white people who don't lie, and Indians who do." They rode in silence a moment, then she continued. "What is your name? What do I call you?"

"Be quiet." He interrupted. "You babble like a little girl and hurt the ears of my pony."

She laughed at him. "That's because I am a little girl."

Wisely, she then shut up and relaxed against his chest.

They rode in silence, following a slight, switchback trail down the mountain. Often they stopped to listen.

Finally, after sitting in silence next to a stream for several minutes, the old Indian spoke to her. "I am Buffalo Shield."

"My name is Beth Mackey, and I'm most pleased to meet you." She glanced up at him. "What manner of Indian are you?"

He stepped off the horse and waited for her to dismount. "I am Kaini. The whites call us Blackfoot, and my home was near Canada on the upper branches of the Great River."

She shrugged. "I've never heard of you. Why are you here, so far from home and your family?"

After drinking from the stream, he led his horse to water. "Drink upstream. We must go."

Complying, she came back and questioned him again. "You didn't answer me. Why are you here?"

"You talk more than your mother," he muttered. Finally, he answered her. "I have no family, they were all killed. Why am I here? I came to kill a man."

She contemplated him for a long moment. "This man must have done something terribly wrong for you to travel all the way from Canada to kill him. Did he kill your family? What did he do?"

"To me?" He shrugged and looked away.

"Nothing."

"The man has done nothing to you, and yet you want to take his life? Well, thank you for helping me get away. But I think the Blackfoot are crazy. Maybe all men."

She watched his expression go from anger, and then sadness, and finally what looked like was resignation. He finally shrugged and answered. "Sometimes I think so."

They rode a few minutes, skirting the White River and moving north. Suddenly, she twisted around and looked at him. "Wait. You saw my mother?"

Sean sat in the dining room of the trading post, eating a stew of mystery meat, undercooked potatoes, and carrots. "What's in this, anyway?"

"You gettin' picky?" Shay had come to sit with him. "Seems to me a hungry man wouldn't be so persnickety."

He speared a piece of meat with his knife, and held it up for inspection. "Catamount? Not strong enough for bear. Not stringy enough for deer meat. Wait a minute. This couldn't be an honest-to-God piece of beef cow, could it?"

Before Shay could answer, there was a commotion from outside, and Ellen strode through the door with all the force of a charging buffalo. She'd changed into clean buckskin pants and tan shirt. Her face had a fresh scrubbed look to it. Sean thought maybe it was red from anger, not scrubbing.

"That woman is always in an all-fired hurry," Shay commented as she spun and did a right flank movement directly at them.

"What are you doing?" she demanded, as she skidded to a stop and glared at them.

"I'm eating some of Shay's wonderful stew," Sean said. "Want some?"

Shay scooted his stool back a bit, to get out of range. When she glanced at him, he held up both hands in surrender. "I'm just watchin' him eat."

Sean could imagine storm clouds forming over her head as he watched her face turn redder than before.

"Shouldn't we be loading pack horses so we can get back on the trail?"

He pretended to think a moment. "Nope. I'm thinking this is a real good spot, right here. As a matter of fact, I'm starting to like this spot real good. What do you think, Mister Shay?"

Ellen's face went from red to white and Shay shook his head. "I'm thinking you two are going to provide me entertainment for years to come."

Her gaze pinned him to his seat. "What?"

Shay decided he was needed somewhere else. "I better go."

Sean pointed his fork at him. "Don't run off, Shay. We still need to talk. Have you seen him lately?"

"Who?" she interjected. "What are you two talking about?"

"No," Shay said, sitting back down. "I haven't. And I should've seen him by now. This is the day he usually comes in."

"As I remember" — he dug into the stew again — "he's a man who likes his rum."

Ellen muttered something very unladylike, stood with her shoulders slumping and her eyes closed a moment, and then sat down at the table. She pulled Sean's bowl to her. Smelling the contents, she turned a little pale, and then pushed it away.

"Would you two mind telling me what's rattling around in those little bitty noggins of yours? Please?"

"Santee," he said, suddenly not interested in the stew. He thought it smelled pretty good, until he saw her turn her nose up at it. Maybe she could do better.

"What? What's a Santee?" She looked to be losing her carefully controlled temper.

"Not a what. Who. I want to see a man named Santee. He ought to be showin' up just any time, now."

Shay, who was watching Ellen, stood and began backing away. "Oh, Lord. . . ."

"Look at her, Shay. She's starting to change color again. I saw a lizard do that once. Prettiest thing I ever saw."

"Have you lost your mind?" Her voice rose in pitch. "My daughter is captive of . . . of . . . God only knows who has her, we don't know if she's alive or dead and you're just sitting here, not a care in the world, waiting to see a man?"

"Well —"

"Damn you, MacLeod. Buffalo Shield already found the trail for us. He's a hell of a lot better on a trail than you —"

"You don't know that." Sean tried to break in, but she ignored him.

"— and he's waiting for us. We should never have left that trail, and we need to get back out there and start searching. Right now. Do you hear me?"

"Did you see that, Shay? She actually stomped her foot." He turned his attention back to her. "Buffalo Shield is a Blackfoot. You've known him two days less than you've known me and suddenly you trust this man? He said there was a trail and you immediately believed him. You're quick to throw over your friends, aren't you?" He looked at her with a level gaze. "He's just as likely to kill me the next time we meet, and then you'll be sold to the French just like your daughter. Is that what you want?"

She looked embarrassed and stuttered. "I . . . you. . . ."

He kept hammering at her. "Look, I know Buffalo Shield doesn't think much of me as a woodsman. You don't either. Hell, nobody does. But, what if he's wrong, which direction do we go? Let's just say he forgets our little truce and we fight. I get lucky and kill Buffalo Shield. Where do we look? There's a lot of trees and brush out there, and I have no desire to run up and down every mountain in this country.

"An old Cree Indian gave me one of the best definitions of confusion I've ever heard and I love to tell it. He told me one of his braves was surprised by an attack and tried to ride away in all directions. That's what has been happening ever since your daughter was taken. It produced nothing and has to end."

She sighed, shook her head, and dropped back in her chair so hard he thought it would break. "You are the most infuriating man I have ever met." She took a couple of deep breaths. "All right. Who's this Santee you're wantin' a reunion with?"

"Now you're asking the right question. I

think a man named Charbonneau may have your daughter. If he's in the area, it just makes sense." He proceeded to give her the short version of how they ran the slaver out of the North Country. "Now, I haven't the foggiest notion where he is. North, south, or who in hell knows. But he's got a sidekick who does know, and that's the man I want to talk to."

"This Santee is the man who likes his rum?" she asked. "And you think he may just wander into this particular post? Of all the posts up and down the river?"

He sat back in his chair, folding his arms across his belly. "Now you got it."

He was amazed to see that she was starting to change color again. "Of all the. . . . What in God's name makes you think . . . ?"

Shay cleared his throat to get their attention. "Speakin' of which." He pointed out the window.

Ellen said, "How did you know . . . ?"

Sean raised his hand, and then at her expression quickly snatched it back. He smiled at her. "Did you know you haven't finished a sentence in several minutes?"

He got the desired result. She was speechless.

The clip-clopping sound of a trotting horse came from outside, and he turned to watch the new arrival as he reined up to the hitching post. Without tying his horse, Santee strode into the store. He was a short man of nondescript looks, unless you call dirty a trait. His full, unkempt beard bore streaks of grey, and the hat he wore looked like he used it for a saddle blanket. His greasy buckskins were stiff with sweat and dirt, and smelled like a barnyard. He wore a belt knife and tomahawk, and he'd left his rifle slung from his saddle. The man walked right by them — his eyes on the bar in the next room.

As soon as Santee entered, he yelled, "Barkeep! Where's the bartender? I need a drink."

Shay started to get up from the table, and Sean put a hand on his arm.

"Let me handle this one, but do me a favor and watch my back. This man is a weasel." As he stood, he smiled. "I need the practice bartending for when I buy you out."

He silently followed the man into the bar and spoke softly. "Hello, Santee."

Santee turned quickly, backing up a step. He looked right and left, and then finally said in a nervous voice, "MacLeod. What are you doing in this country?"

"Oh, I was just passin' through. But then, I talked to some people and heard a story I didn't like too much. It was kind of like the stories we heard on the upper Missouri. I heard a story about some missing girls. Now, you and Charbonneau wouldn't be up to your old tricks again, would you?"

Santee didn't get a chance to answer. Sean heard quick footsteps behind him. As he turned, he was aware of a blur of motion passing him and then Santee hit the floor hard. Just that quick, Ellen was over the top of him and holding a knife to Santee's throat.

"Where is my daughter?" she yelled at him. "Where?"

"I don't know —" Santee started to say. Her knife drew blood.

"Where? Where is your camp?"

Santee had to back-crawl away from the blade. His hand was sneaking toward the knife at his belt, when Sean stepped on his arm.

"Rockingstraw," Santee gasped, surrendering. "We have a camp up on Rockingstraw."

"Are the girls in that camp? Charbonneau has them?"

Santee nodded and Ellen rose from his chest.

"Which side, Santee? Where on Rockingstraw?"

Santee's voice was barely a whisper. "This

side, near the top."

Ellen was up and off the man in an instant and on her way out the door. "You coming, MacLeod?"

He stood waiting as Santee rose slowly to his feet. "I'll be just a minute. Santee, I'm trying really hard to think of a reason not to kill you. If you want to live you'll do something for me. I assume you'll want to live through this?"

"Sure, I'll. . . ."

He stared at the man a moment while he tried to think of everything that could go wrong in this situation. He'd been through too many scrapes to think everything always went as planned.

"Santee, I'm betting your bunch of slavers will scatter if attacked. I'm also betting you have plans for that. What happens when you split up? Where is your rendezvous point?"

"I don't —"

He backhanded Santee and blood flew across the mirror behind the bar. "Don't lie to me."

Santee straightened, wiping blood from his nose and wiping his hand on his shirt. "If we're attacked, everyone grabs a girl. We're supposed to escape going different directions. A few miles from here the White River flows into the Black. There's a small settlement there and that's where we'll meet. We wait three days from when we scatter, then make our way on down to the Mississip' and finally New Orleans. That's unless someone from New Orleans meets us first with a paddleboat. They are always pretty anxious for what we bring. That's all I know, MacLeod."

He looked distastefully at Santee. "Mister Shay. If you'll instruct the good Captain Frane that Santee will lead him and his merry men to Rockingstraw Mountain, I'd appreciate it. Give him one drink now, and one before they leave. If he doesn't cooperate, kill him." He looked hard at Shay. "And, I mean that."

Shay shrugged and said, "Consider it done. Hell, I may do it, anyway. The bastard."

"Santee, you'd better pray that girl is alive. If she isn't, I won't kill you. I'll let Missus Mackey have you. Do you understand?"

Santee backed up against the bar. "I need that drink."

FIFTEEN

Sean stepped outside and saw immediately that Shay wouldn't have to tell the soldiers. It was also obvious that she must have alerted the army before she came to see them in the post.

Captain Frane leaned close, talking to Ellen. She was nodding her head and agreeing with him. Frane reached out and pulled her to him and she didn't resist. He couldn't tell if the embrace was entirely voluntary, but she didn't fight it. The sight of her body tight against his was more than he could take.

"What the hell?" Sean said as he walked up to them. As soon as he advanced, so did the soldiers. He counted over twenty men as they stepped toward him.

Ellen stepped quickly away from the captain and wouldn't meet Sean's eyes.

"Ellen?" he asked. "What's going on?"

The men edged closer and with his hand

on his fighting knife, he spoke harshly. "Captain, if your boys in blue get any closer to me they're going to get a lot of red on their pretty blue shirts."

Lazily holding up his hand, and with a smirk on his face, he stopped the soldiers' forward movement. "Mister MacLeod, the army is much better equipped to handle this rescue than some itinerant trader. Ellen agrees with me and will guide us to the proper mountain. She'll also assist in finding the campsite where the captives are held."

He couldn't believe what he heard and still couldn't get her to look at him. "Ellen, talk to me. What are you doing?"

The captain interrupted again. "As the commander of this post, I'm ordering you to stay away from her and this situation. Any interference from you and we'll put you in leg irons."

He stood for a moment trying to control his breathing. "Do you know what Charbonneau looks like? Do you know how many men he has? Do you know anything? Where will they go if you flush them out and they run? Will they take the captives with them? Kill them?"

"MacLeod, please," she pleaded, still not looking at him. "There's no need for you to risk yourself now. You're just one man. We know where they are. The army will get them back."

"Just like the army found them? This strutting peacock couldn't find his ass with both hands." She made no reply. He heard Shay in the background cursing. "So, that's it? You're just going to sashay up the trail and make the rescue? Today?"

"MacLeod, you're wasting our time. Your concerns are groundless. For your information, we'll travel until dark and then bivouac. Leaving the camp in the early hours of the morning, we'll get positioned and attack at dawn, when they're still asleep. The only casualties will be on their side."

Ellen turned and had one foot in a stirrup when Sean spoke softly. "A simple thank you would have been nice." When she didn't answer, he gave her his final thoughts. "I thought we had a little something going. My mistake. Does betrayal come so easy to you?"

Her shoulders hunched and she leaned her head against the saddle a moment. Mounting, she turned to look at him for the first time. With tears in her eyes, she said. "We've only known each other three days, MacLeod. Three damned days. I don't owe you anything." She shook her head, wiping away the tears. "Damn you."

Sean led Thunder to the corral and stripped off the riding gear and packs. Rubbing the horse between the ears, he said, "You're going to get fat and lazy if we stay here much longer."

"What about Santee?" Shay asked.

"Lock him in a storeroom or something. Make sure he doesn't get away."

He strolled back to the post and entered the bar. A few of the townsmen were there and ignored him. Shay came over to his table carrying a jug and a couple of mugs.

"A toast to the good captain and his merry men," Shay said with a smirk.

He raised his mug. "To hell with them."

"It really isn't any of your responsibility, you know."

"My thought, exactly," he said, staring into the bottom of his mug. "I have other things to do."

Shay's voice was sympathetic. "There's nothing you could do about it. Once in a great while things are beyond our control. We just have to accept it."

"Yep. There's nothing we can do about it."

"I don't know what's got into that girl. I thought we knew her." Shay paused a moment, and then looked askance at him. "You could fight for her, you know. Let her know you're interested."

He filled his mug again, and then replied morosely, "It takes two, Shay. I didn't see a bit of interest on her part. When she thought I could help, she was all on my side. Once I gave her what she needed to know, she jumped ship and went with that pompous ass who calls himself a captain commander of the army."

After a moment, Shay responded softly. "You know he's been sparkin' the girl for a while. The world didn't start when you rode in. She's never given him aye or nay that I know of. I still say she's a good woman with a lot on her mind. You can't expect her to start something romantic while trying to save her daughter."

"She made her choice today, seems to me. Like I said, it didn't take her long to jump on his little bandwagon." He shrugged. "Ah, what the hell. She said it best. I only met her three days ago. The only thing is, she looks like my late wife and I guess I made some assumptions that weren't right. My mistake."

Shay got up and left. When he returned moments later, he had two plates. "Beef and beans, with a bit of bread to build up your strength. Tomorrow will be a better day, and then the next she'll be back. You can settle it with her then."

He was feeling the effects of the rum and was glad to have a meal. "You really believe that?"

"Well, I do believe with a bit of luck she'll be back day after tomorrow. Do I believe they'll make a rescue? That bunch?" Shay shook his head. "Not a chance in hell."

Later that evening Sean sat on the landing in front of the store, thinking of Ellen and Captain Frane in camp together. Sitting close. Whispering to each other. He wished he'd been a little more forceful when they were together, but realized he didn't really know what his feelings were. The problem was, he felt drawn to her and worried that maybe he was a moth and she the flame. The other thing? He shouldn't have opened up to her the way he had. He was too trusting way too soon. Now she knew just about everything there was to know about him. He'd have to watch that in the future.

Still running possibilities around the trails in his mind, he saw someone coming out of the long shadows along the trail. Little puffballs of dust rose from each step of the horse, but there was no cadence and the horse seemed to stumble once before the rider pulled up its head.

Shay came to stand beside him, shading his eyes with his hand against the setting sun. "Well, I'll be damned. That's Ellen's little girl, Beth. But, who's that Indian?"

"That, my friend, is the man who's supposed to kill me."

Shay just stared with his mouth open.

Sean watched as Buffalo Shield rode up to them with Beth sitting in front of him. They both looked tired and his pony looked like it was about to drop from the extra weight.

"I brought the little one home."

The girl swung her leg over the horse's drooping head, and then dropped lightly to the ground. She immediately turned to the Indian. Ellen was right. She was an image of her mother, and they both had a striking resemblance to Angie. Her voice was melodious and showed more energy than anyone else possessed.

"Thank you, Grandfather. You will always have a place in my heart."

Sean's eyebrows went up and Buffalo Shield's eyes stonily met his. Grandfather was a term of respect in most tribes for older warriors. For the life of him, he couldn't imagine this bloodthirsty warrior evoking that kind of tenderness from the young girl.

They led them inside the post and sat at a table. Any townsmen there fled quickly at the sight of the Indian.

Beth asked for her mother and Shay's wife took her into another room, clucking and fussing with her.

While putting away three plates of food, Buffalo Shield told them of the rescue. "Tonight I heard much firing from up the mountain. Many rifles."

Sean lunged up, only to be brought back with Shay's hand on his arm. "It's nearly dark, Sean. You can't do anything now. We'll have to wait."

Buffalo Shield looked at him, waiting for an explanation. "Beth's mother went with the army to rescue the girls, hoping her daughter would be with them. They were going to camp on the mountain tonight and attack the slaver's position at dawn."

The Indian snorted, but didn't say anything. He didn't have to. Most Indians preferred attacking at dawn, to catch their quarry unaware. But a good ambush can be carried out anytime and Captain Frane would be blissfully unaware of his surroundings.

They all turned as a shriek came from the

other room. Beth came rushing in.

"My mother? Where's my mother?"

Shay held his hands out, trying to calm her. "Ellen is with the army, heading up the mountain and hoping to rescue you and the rest of the girls."

Beth shook her head. "No. I heard them talking and they'll just split up and run away. They won't catch them there." She looked around desperately, and then focused on Buffalo Shield. "You have to take me back, Grandfather. We have to find her."

Buffalo Shield, looking like a tired old man, was struggling to his feet when Sean spoke quietly. "No."

When the tired Indian gratefully settled back down, Sean spoke to both of them. "Buffalo Shield, you're worn out and rightfully so. I'd like you to stay here and protect the girl. I'll go." Beth wouldn't need protecting in the post, but he surprised himself by wanting to give the Indian a way to save face. Another thought came unbidden to his mind. The Osage.

"Shay, I think you can trust Buffalo Shield." The Indian looked at him incredulously. "With the patrol out, and some of the townsmen gone with them, you're shorthanded here. The Osage may choose this moment to attack. If I were you, I'd have Buffalo Shield scout around and watch. He can be your early warning if anything is afoot. In the meantime, you need to prepare for an attack. Just in case."

He turned to Beth, who was following the quick exchange, and said gently. "You don't know me, but I'm a friend of your mother's."

With the alacrity of a child's mind, she immediately hit on the one spot he didn't want to talk about. "You're her friend and you let her go alone?"

"She's not alone, Beth. She went with Captain Frane and the army."

"Frane?" Beth hooted. "That pompous ass?"

Sean grinned at Shay, who just rolled his eyes.

"It was her choice, girl," Sean told her. "Not mine. However, it's a decision I'm beginning to regret and I'm going to rectify it as soon as possible."

"Will you bring her back to me?"

"I shall."

Sean realized he'd made the same promise to the mother and that hadn't turned out well. Beth was back, but through no action of his own.

He was lost in thought when he realized Shay was standing beside him.

"What are you thinking, lad? You're going alone and the odds aren't good."

Sean grinned at him. "You ever study history?"

"Actually, I had good schooling before I tired of the headmaster's bullying and came west. Much to my parent's remorse, I might add. Why? Are you going to teach me some history?"

"No, I wouldn't presume to do that. I was just thinking of a quote that King Henry is supposed to have said on the eve of the Battle of Agincourt."

"Where six thousand English archers defeated thirty thousand Frenchmen? I remember. They had bows like yours, and the men to pull them. So, your thoughts?"

Sean looked out the window into the gloom. "The night is swiftly leaving and the battle is on the morn." He then turned and looked at Shay, and in a sad voice, finished the quote. "And an old man's a pitiful thing, indeed."

He could feel the man's gaze on his back as he walked out.

Going through the door, he heard Buffalo Shield mutter, *"Hoka Hey."* Sean thought that was from the language of the plains Indians to the west, but couldn't argue with the sentiment. It was a good day to die.

Sixteen

Sean slept fitfully and the dreams came again. Waking abruptly an hour before dawn, he stood and walked to the door of the livery. The cool morning breeze dried the sweat from his forehead. The sound of horses and mules stirring around came to him and he walked over to the corral. Standing at the pole fence, he wasn't surprised when Thunder nudged his shoulder.

"You're spoiled," he said as he fed the horse a small apple. "Be ready, boy. We've got a lot to do this day."

Thinking of the night, he wondered if the dreams were some kind of warning for what lay ahead. The fighting and screaming, figures leaping through fire, and flights of arrows that blackened the sky. He never understood it, but always woke charged up and ready to do battle. He'd have to ask Buffalo Shield about it, if he lived. Maybe the old medicine man would have some answers.

He stood working on his weapons while chewing on a piece of jerky and sensed someone moving up to him. From the size and silhouette, he knew who it was and half expected a knife in the ribs.

"The captives will not be there." Buffalo Shield's voice was gruff. "Your journey may be long."

"I'm not going for the captives. If that makes me a bad person, so be it. I have to check on Beth's mom. I have to see, if for no other reason than Beth will know and have closure."

It was getting lighter and he could see the other man clearly.

"You have to know what happened to the woman. Your heart is with her?"

He shrugged, not knowing what to say. He'd been up and down that trail in his mind and couldn't see a clear answer. And he thought the answer might scare him more than the coming battle.

The Indian took Sean's longbow off the saddle and looked at it a moment. Trying to pull it, he could only bring it halfway to his ear. "Much bow. You can use this?"

"I do, although it's starting to hurt my shoulder some. It's called an English longbow."

Pulling an arrow from the quiver on Sean's saddle, he compared it to one he pulled from his own. The arrow from Sean's pouch was half again as long. "Show me."

Looking at the man a moment, he finally took the arrow and nocked it. Buffalo Shield pointed to a deer browsing close to the compound, about fifty yards away. "Meat."

Smoothly, Sean pulled and released. The metal-tipped arrow left with a hissing sound, and then went completely though the small doe and shattered on a rock beyond. The deer leaped straight up, and then after taking a couple of steps went to its knees. It fell over kicking in the leaves.

Buffalo Shield grunted. "Know this. The Osage may have allied with the slavers and will be waiting for you. Use that against them, before they get into range with their bows. They will not understand." Walking toward the slain deer, the Indian turned to him once more. "Stay alive, Ghostrider. We still have to meet. There must be blood."

"Yep." Almost like an incantation, Sean repeated, "There must be blood."

Mounting Thunder, Sean left the compound and headed down the trail. His mind was full of thoughts about his slain wife, his feelings for Ellen and guilt for wanting — needing to love again. Confused thoughts rattled around in his head until foam splattered on his face from Thunder's mouth.

Cursing, he reined in the horse and noticed the animal's entire body was covered in foam and sweat. He immediately dismounted, giving Thunder a chance to regain his strength. He'd pushed too hard. For the first time this morning, it registered where he was. The other day, it seemed like a lifetime ago, it took about three hours to make the fork in the trail. If he wasn't mistaken, he'd cut the three hours to two and the junction of trails should be just over the hill.

He let the horse cool a few minutes more and then led him to a nearby stream to drink. He allowed his mount to drink only for a moment before he pulled him away. Too much water would be as bad as not enough. He walked Thunder toward the crest of the hill, stopping him well short so only Sean's head was visible over the top. His eyes narrowed as he took in the scene below.

The rescue party hadn't made it up the mountain. Hell, they hadn't even made it to the mountain. No sound came from the forest and there wasn't any movement that he could see. It looked like they'd been ambushed just as they turned west toward the mountain trail. The location wasn't far from the spot he and Ellen had spent the night.

Finally, he mounted and rode down the hill into the natural bowl surrounded by forest and fern. He slowly made his way along the trail, looking for Ellen. The bodies were scattered and stripped of weapons. The horses were gone. From their placement, it looked as if the army patrol had tried to run away. Most were hit with rifle balls, but a few had arrow wounds. He could see where someone had walked among the wounded and dispatched them with a hatchet. They were scalped, but not mutilated.

Buffalo Shield was right. The rifle balls spoke of Charbonneau's men, the arrows and scalping of the Osage.

The hair stood up on his neck. With the Osage involved, the problem became much worse.

He rode among them with his rifle at the ready, half his attention on the bodies and half on the forest. After searching twice, he couldn't find Ellen and realized her worst nightmare had happened.

Movement at the edge of the clearing caught his attention and he leaped off his horse and rolled up behind a log. Slowly,

Red Eagle and two more Cherokee rode into the clearing. He stood and watched them approach.

The Cherokee sat his horse while the others looked around. "We did not do this."

Sean shrugged, anxious to leave. "I didn't figure you did. This has Osage written all over it. Unfortunately, others may not hold that view."

"What will you do?"

He looked at the Indian and shrugged, thinking of Ellen and the job ahead. "Only thing I can do. Go after them. They have Missus Mackey."

"If they've taken a white woman, it will be war with the whites. All the tribes will be blamed." Red Eagle shook his head. "I'm sorry to say this. If they have her, she won't last long. It's too risky for them to keep her."

"I know." He was lost in thought a moment. "Look, I need you to do something for me. It's dangerous, but will help me and may also change the way the whites think of the Cherokee."

At Red Eagle's nod, he continued. "I have information that they will scatter soon and meet up where the White River flows into the Black. They will have the girls there so they can load them on boats and sell them later. I need you to go to the post and talk to Rob Shay. Let him know what has happened here. Then get together as many men as possible and try to beat the slavers to that rendezvous point. You'll have to hurry. This is coming to a head very quickly."

The Cherokee nodded. "We can do that. What will you do?"

Sean was busy tucking his pant legs inside the knee-length moccasins he wore, then wrapping them with strips of hide to keep them there. He did the same with the cuffs of his shirt, although more loosely so it wouldn't impede movement. He hung his pack on the horse, leaving himself with a powder horn and shot bag, plus his bow and a quiver full of arrows. His fighting knife and tomahawk were slung on his belt. He was as ready as he'd ever be.

"Like I said, I'm going after the woman. If I'm lucky, I can get her away from them. If we're really lucky and they're in a hurry to get away, they won't spend much time looking for us."

"If you're not lucky?"

He shrugged. "Then we're dead and it doesn't matter."

As they were getting ready to leave, he led Thunder over to Red Eagle. "My horse is played out. I ran him too hard. Take him to Shay. I'll travel these hills faster on foot."

The Cherokee reached down and shook his hand. "Good luck. We'll do our part."

He had a sudden thought that made him grin. "One more thing. Rob Shay is holding a man named Santee. If he would accidentally leave the cell door open and let Santee escape, the man might lead you to Charbonneau and the girls. It might be a bit of insurance just in case the man lied to us. He's not exactly trustworthy. I'd put a couple of your men on him and watch where he goes. He may lead them to where you're going, or somewhere else entirely. If he doesn't lead to the girls, you know what to do. Don't get into any kind of battle if you can avoid it, just get those girls."

"Anything else?" The Cherokee shook his head and smiled. "Like a last will and testament?"

Sean had forgotten the man was educated. He smiled. "Yes, as a matter of fact there is. All I own goes to the little girl, Beth. Shay will know what to do."

As the Cherokee rode away he heard him mutter, "Damn, man. I wasn't serious."

After looking a moment at the map Shay had provided, Sean turned and started up the trail. He tried to set a measured pace, but soon found his lungs burning as he went faster. Realizing he was doing the same to himself as he had done to his horse, he alternated between walking and running.

It was still mid-morning and the sun hadn't burned off the mist rising from the cold water of the river. The air was cool and fresh. Now that he wasn't running so hard, he could hear something besides the pounding in his ears. From ahead of him came the shrill piping of quail along with magpie, and the fussing of a wren in the bushes. Numerous deer rubs showed on the trees, and overturned deadfalls gave evidence of deer and bear. Off the trail a few yards, he saw the half-eaten carcass of a small deer and knew a mountain lion would be back for it later, if the coyotes didn't get it first.

Most of the trail had been going gradually uphill for two hours and he'd covered several miles. The path went around the mountain. His only hope was that the slavers had made camp last night and celebrated their victory. If they were drunk enough, maybe they'd sleep late this morning and he could gain some ground.

He was starting into a clearing when, about fifty yards ahead, a rabbit scurried from under a bush. He left the path in a long dive. Careful to make no noise, nor shake the elderberry bushes he'd crouched under, he moved forward, skirting the clearing.

At the other end of the clearing, the trail forked. The main trail went on around the mountain, while the smaller and seldom used trail went up higher on the ridge. Two men hid beyond the fork of the trail, one Osage and the other looked like a trapper. If he'd been riding a horse, they would have heard him coming and sprung their trap.

Silently, avoiding looking directly at them, he approached from the side, unlimbering the longbow. He had no doubts what the men would do to him if they captured him.

His first arrow took the Osage through the heart, the metal point slicing through his ribs. The trapper, hearing the Indian grunt, turned to look and took an arrow through his body. He toppled trying to reach his musket, which fell to the side.

Sean stepped on the man's hand as it reached the gun, and then kicked the musket out of reach. With a quick look around, he figured these two were supposed to ambush anyone following the slavers. If it were a big party of men, then they would continue hiding and report the trail taken by the rescuers. A simple plan . . . foiled by a rabbit.

The trapper's hoarse breathing brought

him back to the matter at hand. He knelt and could see his arrow had gone through his lungs. By his gurgling breath, the man didn't have long.

He tugged on the arrow and the pain caused the man to focus on him. "You took a woman when you ambushed the army. Is she still alive?"

"You go to hell," the man said with blood bubbling on his lips.

Sean dropped his knee on the man's chest and the trapper screamed in pain. "Tell me about the woman."

When the man could speak, he said, "The Osage wanted the woman, but the Frenchie Charbonneau took a likin' to her. He set a couple of men to guard her from the Indians. She was ok when we left early this morning."

"Where are they?"

The trapper tried to answer, but coughed weakly and then choked on his blood. The man was gone before he could answer.

Retrieving his arrow from the Osage body, he put it in his quiver. The arrow lodged in the trapper's chest had snapped when he dropped his knee on him. That left him with nineteen arrows. Once the battle joined, he couldn't afford to miss.

He took the trail that went up the mountain. The vegetation cleared somewhat the higher he went, revealing some of the country below. The going was slower, but he felt he was gaining ground if the slavers were on the lower trail. After an hour of travel, he stopped to take a breather.

The country opened up before him as he stood on a sheer bluff of limestone. Several hundred feet below, parts of the other trail appeared from under the canopy. Slightly to his right, he discerned movement. With a hard push, he thought he could get ahead of the slavers as long as the trail held out. Quietly, and keeping out of sight in the trees, he ran.

When shadows were turning long, and it was getting difficult to see in the gloom of the forest, he figured it was about an hour before sundown. Darkness would come quickly under the trees. He descended to the lower trail. He'd kept abreast of the slavers all afternoon. With the children holding them back, it had been easy and afforded him some rest.

The slavers camped in a clearing on the side of a large spring. Water burbling out of the ground formed a large pool and then flowed down a short incline into a stream that headed east. Men yelled at each other over the noise of the spring. He was surprised they'd camped in such a noisy place, but they probably felt safe enough given the number of sentries they had out.

Sean lay on his belly among a clump of forest fern, watching them prepare the camp. Once the camp was set, they brought the captives forward and made them sit on one side of the main fire. They tied them on a tether that went from around their waists to a long rope. No one could run without taking the rest of the captives with them.

Two men brought Ellen in separately. Her shoulders slumped in defeat, and she shuffled forward and then dropped when one of the men pushed her down.

In the dim light, it looked like her face was either smudged or bruised, and a rip down the side of her shirt exposed her arm to the shoulder. He almost rose when an Indian came over to look at her. The Osage reached down to grab her arm when a shout came from across the camp.

Charbonneau stood pointing his rifle at the Indian. Finally, the man rose and walked away while Ellen sat with her head between her knees.

Men came in carrying a couple of small deer. They made short work of skinning the animals, and their haunches sizzled over large fires in moments. The slight breeze blew his way, bringing him the scent of the venison. He hoped the growl of his own stomach wouldn't alert the sentries. The girls and Ellen were given fresh water skins filled at the spring. As he watched, they fed the captives and then led them off in a line to the bushes to take care of their needs. A few minutes later, they brought them back to the clearing, but closer to the trees where they bedded down for the night. The captives didn't have blankets. It looked like the girls were used to it and they just curled up and appeared to go to sleep. Ellen sat slumped with her back to a tree.

A commotion on the other side of the clearing got his attention as an Indian came running up to report to one of the Osage and to Charbonneau. The Frenchman immediately put more sentries out and stood looking around at the forest. Finally appearing satisfied, the slaver went to his blankets.

Rob Shay watched the Cherokee, Red Eagle, ride into the compound of Jones Mill leading Sean MacLeod's horse. He felt a quick moisture in his eyes and quickly wiped his hand across his face. Ellen's daughter was inside helping with the noon meal and he was grateful for that.

Red Eagle stopped in front of him while

one of his men turned the extra horse into the corral. They'd done business before so they knew each other, at least by name.

The Indian must have seen the expression on his face, because he smiled and said, "Your friend was alive when I last saw him, although he was heading into a lot of trouble." The man went on to explain what they'd seen about the ambush and where it happened. "Ghostrider thinks the woman is alive and has gone after her. He's probably right, but who knows how long that will stay true."

"Maybe we can get together some more men and go help," Shay said, as he looked around the mostly empty compound.

"No," Red Eagle said, shaking his head. "He left instructions for us."

"What?"

The Indian grinned at him. "You need to let the man Santee escape. I'll have a couple of men follow him in case he leads us to a different rendezvous than what he's told you. I'll get all the men we can get together and try and beat this Frenchman with his captives to the place where the White flows into the Black River."

"Sounds like you've got your work cut out for you. I'll see if I can get some help for you."

"No," Red Eagle said sharply. "I know you want to help, but it's better this way. The Ghostrider will take care of the white woman. The rest are Indian girls. We will take care of that problem."

Shay's mind went immediately to how jumpy the settlers and army were. A battle of any kind could lead to misunderstandings. "That may start a war."

"The war has already started. You just don't know it yet. The Osage allied with the French slaver Charbonneau. They have killed your people and your soldiers. Soon, the Osage will move on your post. Spend your time preparing for that. We'll help if we can, but there are a lot of Osage and very few Cherokee."

"All right." He didn't see much else he could do. "When your men are ready, have them stop by the post for supplies. We can at least do that for you. I have plenty of powder and shot, with extra rifles. Take what you need."

The Indian nodded and rode away. Shay went back inside and stopped to talk to his partner, Nathan Jones. Jones took the news calmly.

"It'll work out, Rob. We have many friends. The way things are going, it looks like Mister MacLeod would have been a great help to General Washington a few years ago. He'd make a good general himself." Jones smiled a humorless smile. "Now, let me go feed the prisoner. I'm not used to that sort of thing, and I might accidentally leave his cell door open. Then, we'll leave his fate to the Cherokee."

Rob Shay shuddered as he thought about that. Then, he went inside to break the news to his wife and Beth. They had a lot of work to do.

SEVENTEEN

The gibbous moon hung low on the horizon when Sean made his way to the camp below. Darkness covered the forest like a shroud and he moved slowly, using that darkness for cover. Before the sun had set he'd chosen his route, going over it several times in his mind. His path took him directly toward one of the outlying sentries. The guard was a trapper and he hoped the man wouldn't be as alert as his Osage counterparts. He smoked a pipe constantly and Sean could find him in the darkness just by the smell. The journey took almost an hour, and by then the rising moon cast faint shadows in the forest. He could see just enough.

The limestone rocks were still warm from the day's heat as he leaned on his hand to skirt the boulders close to the camp. Any sound would alert the sentry. The rubbing of buckskin on a bush or dislodging a rock would be a giveaway. The sounds coming from the huge spring helped cover his approach, but any noise out of the ordinary would alert the guard. The sentry turned toward him and he dropped his face to the leaves so the distant firelight wouldn't reflect in his eyes. The guard rubbed his eyes and looked like he was trying to stay awake. Finally, the man turned and faced the camp.

Sean made no sound as his arm snaked around the man's throat, cutting off his air as his blade slid between the sentry's ribs. The man stiffened and tried to throw him off, but quickly lost his strength as Sean let him slump gently to the ground.

The girls were asleep, but Ellen was awake and looking around. Had she heard some small sound? Starting toward her, and wondering how to get her attention without raising the whole camp, he froze as an Indian rose slowly from his blankets close to the fire. Sean recognized him as the same Osage Charbonneau warned away from Ellen earlier in the evening.

The Indian stood a moment, looking around at the camp. Apparently satisfied no one was awake, he moved quietly toward Ellen, stopping for a moment to speak to one of the Osage sentries. Sean thought he was on a call of nature when he walked right past Ellen. Just as he went out of sight of the camp, the Indian abruptly reached back and, putting a hand over Ellen's mouth, jerked her off the ground and back into the foliage.

Sean moved.

Ellen kicked and scratched at the man as he carried her farther into the trees, but the Indian was huge and it had little effect. Finally, about fifty steps from the camp, he threw her on the ground, taking the rest of her torn blouse away in his hand.

Sean had never seen such a look of stark terror on the face of anyone as she backpedaled frantically, digging her heels into the forest floor, trying to get away and panting in her fear. He thought instantly of what it must have been like for Angie. Ellen screamed once, hoarse and anguished, but he was sure no one would hear her cry over the sound of the springs.

He couldn't wait anymore and threw his tomahawk, his anger adding strength to the throw. The blade cut deeply into the Indian's back, but missed the spine. The Osage arched in pain, and then turned around toward him, pulling his own knife. Sean walked in on him and, slapping the weakened Indian's knife hand aside, sent his own blade into the man's belly, cutting up and over in a figure seven. His rage was so great the man was lifted off his feet before he fell limply back to the ground.

Ellen's eyes were wide in astonishment and her mouth still gaped open in a silent scream. Retrieving his ax, he settled it and his knife back in his belt. Turning to Ellen, he reached for her. "Ellen, we have to move."

She just sat there, paralyzed with fear and apparently not hearing him, staring at the dead Indian. He realized she couldn't see his face in the dark gloom of the forest. In her mind, he may as well have been one of the trappers come to fight over her and one nightmare may have been traded for another.

Her grabbed her and pulled her struggling body to him, turning her away from the dead Indian. "Ellen, it's Sean."

She was suddenly clutching him with inhuman strength. "Sean? Oh, God. Sean?"

They held the embrace, crushing their bodies together for a couple of minutes while he whispered in her ear, trying to comfort her. Finally, she backed from him and picked up her blouse. It was ripped beyond repair. All she had on was a thin chemise to cover her breasts.

Quickly, he stripped off his buckskin shirt and put it on her. It was big, but he cut the arms of the shirt off and then tied the shirttail around her waist. It would have to do.

He led off with her close behind. After they'd gone another hundred paces, she reached out and grabbed him.

"The girls?"

"No time." He knew what she wanted.

"What? We can't leave them."

He could see her stubbornness bulling up for a major argument so he held her by the shoulders and quickly explained, with his mouth next to her ear to cut down on noise. "We'll have to leave them for a while. I'm hoping the slavers won't look for us very long. Those girls are his money makers and I think Charbonneau will be in a hurry getting them to market. If things work out, we have a surprise for them when they do."

Making a slow half-circle around the camp, he found the trail. Once he found it, he turned perpendicular to it and went downhill into the forest.

"Can't we make better time if we used the trail?" Ellen's voice was quiet as she stepped close to him.

"They'll be all over the trail at daybreak. Plus, some of them have horses and would run us down. We don't need to go far. Help me look for a place to hide. We'll be better off if we go to ground and don't leave tracks for them to see in the morning."

She looked doubtful so he tried to explain. "Look, we've done the first thing they'll expect when we went downhill. That's the first thing someone does if they're trying to get away. Downhill is faster and easier. The second thing they'll expect is for us to take the trail. Smart money says to run as fast and far as possible, and then try and hide. By then, we'll be tired and if they find us, easily defeated. I'm hoping that going to ground immediately will fool them. At least until they get tired of looking."

She studied him a moment, and then sighed. "All right."

His head snapped around at her, trying to see her expression. That had to be the first time she'd agreed with him about anything.

They found shelter an hour later. With the occasional glow from lightning, provided by an early morning thunderstorm marching by in the distance, he found a lichen-covered boulder jutting out over the slope. Walking around it and parting the bushes in front of it revealed a hollowed out space beneath the overhang. He took a stick and poked around as far as he could reach, trying to make sure nothing waited inside.

Finally, knife in hand, he advanced into the small cave under the rock. Once inside, he struck his flint into some tinder and the small fire showed an elbow in the cave that went back a few feet. Sticks and sand covered the floor but nothing else to worry about that he could see. He was glad it was late spring. Otherwise the small cave might have a black bear in residence.

First he laid his rifle and bow within easy reach, and then reaching out, pulled Ellen inside and sat with his back to the wall. With the sharp turn in the cave entrance, a cursory glance would reveal nothing but darkness to anyone outside.

He pulled Ellen to his chest, hugging her close. She leaned back and then started shaking. He could tell she was crying. When she started to say something, he said softly. "Rest, don't talk."

Her anguished voice came in a whisper. "I didn't find Beth. She wasn't with them. I'm afraid. . . ."

He covered her mouth with his hand, speaking swiftly to her. "She's safe. Beth got away somehow. Buffalo Shield found her and brought her in."

Ellen gasped and tried to turn around to face him, already forming more questions. He spun her away again, and held her.

"I was afraid we'd find her dead, like the Osage girl."

He just stroked her hair and shoulders until she settled down.

Once they were still, she sighed and snuggled deeper into his arms. Surprised, he leaned his head forward into her hair. Soon, fatigue overtook him and he slept with no dreams. At least, not bad ones.

Sean woke slowly, with just a bare hint of light coming in through the cave opening. His hands were under her shirt and cupping her breasts, and he could feel her nipples hard under his palms. When he tried to move his hands, she groaned in protest and murmured something about being warm, as she held her arms over his. Chuckling, he knew why his dreams weren't bad during the night. He relented for a few moments, enjoying the closeness and softly kneading her flesh. She moaned as he nuzzled her neck softly.

He expected visions of Angie to fill his mind, along with guilt, but it didn't happen. When he tried, he couldn't remember any guilt with Willow. Maybe time did heal and he wouldn't feel he was disrespecting her memory. It was time to move on. Finally, the cramp in his back decided the situation for him.

"Ellen, I have to move. My back has a cramp and my bladder's about to bust."

She relented and scooted to the side, while he made his way to the cave entrance. He waited, listening intently. Every sound he could hear outside seemed normal, so he decided to chance it. Their little cave wasn't that far from the slaver's campsite, although he was sure their camp would move this morning.

Outside the cave, which was little more than a cutout under the massive outcropping of stone, he stretched while watching for any movement. Looking around, he saw they couldn't have been luckier. Dense growth surrounded the top of the outcropping and, looking to both sides, their refuge didn't look any different than the other rocks and boulders along the ridge. Looking on down the mountain, he could see another ridge like the one they were on, and then a river. Hopefully, it was the White and they could follow it back to the post.

The only thing in the immediate vicinity was a woodchuck ambling among the rocks looking for roots. The excavation of its den was a few feet away, and he watched the animal closely. A few moments later, a couple of immature woodchucks appeared out of the burrow. Apparently the animals had accepted them as part of the local denizens, but normally the animal was easily startled.

He stepped to the backside of the rock and relieved himself, intending to cover the traces with a scattering of soil from the den close by.

Ellen hurriedly pushed him away as soon as he finished and squatted over the same spot. She looked at him with a small smile and he suddenly realized he was still exposed. He hastily put himself away.

"Nice, MacLeod. Not bad at all." When she saw him turning red, she laughed softly. "Do you think those men from the camp, especially the Osage, were so modest?" She finished and stood, scooting leaves over the spot with her foot. She came to stand by him. "What now?"

He shrugged. "We wait and hide. They may realize we're hiding, but they'll be looking at bigger caves or blowdown areas, like deadfalls. I'm hoping they won't take much time. There's a good chance our little hole in the ground won't be noticed. If we try to get away now, we'll surely be seen. I don't think they'll search for more than a day."

Ellen just looked at him a moment and he couldn't decipher her expression. "I'm not worried. Not at all. Remember, I've seen you fight."

He took her hand and pulled her back toward the cave.

They were momentarily startled by a rustling in the forest. The largest woodchuck froze, ready to scurry back into its den. The young ones were frozen statues mimicking the adult. They were both relieved when several turkeys blundered into the clearing, and it seemed to drive his point home.

Ellen stared at the turkeys and breathed softly. "I'm hungry."

"Sorry, not today. Between the whistle pigs and the turkeys, we have enough sentinels to alert the whole countryside. Besides, we really don't want to spook those turkeys. If they fly up, it'd sound like a runaway wagon rolling down the mountain. And we can't chance a fire. Maybe tomorrow." He reached into a pouch at his side and came out with some jerky. "This will have to do."

"Do you have a water bag?" When he shook his head, she handed the dried meat back. "You'll just have to listen to my stomach growl. This will just make us thirsty. Listening to the river below will be torture."

Her voice faded, and he watched her eyes widen as she stared at his bare chest. Stepping up to him, she gently turned him as she ran her finger along the angry red knife wound on his side. She looked up at him with a questioning expression.

"A few nights ago, an Indian jumped me. We had quite a little fracas for a while. It's healing."

"You have so many scars." Her breath was warm on his chest as she came close to him. "Too many scars."

"We'd better get under cover before someone comes lookin' this direction." Pushing her gently, they knelt and crawled back into the small cave.

He lay down with his back against the wall, so he could at least see partially outside. Taking off his buckskin shirt, Ellen spread it on the floor of the cave, and then reclined next to him. She lay there in her thin chemise and he couldn't take his gaze from her. Finally, she reached for him and he kissed her.

After a couple of minutes he pulled back, leaving her panting and staring at him. "We can't do this. Not now."

"I want you to. You know I've been married. I've even been captured, raped, and survived. It's not like you're protecting my virtue. I thought you wanted me."

"Just like that? What about your friend,

the great and late Captain Frane? You were quick enough to go off with him," he said in a harsh voice, and then glanced outside, startled at the amount of noise he'd made.

Recognizing the need for quiet, her voice was a whisper in his ear. "I'm sorry about that. But dammit, I was desperate. It was shameless of me. I knew the captain wanted me, but I didn't want him. Hell, Beth doesn't even like him. But I did consider it. I shouldn't have, but I did. It's not easy for a woman alone. Then everything came apart when I walked into the tavern and you were there. . . . I've never felt like that before."

He remembered that day and the hollow feeling he experienced when he saw her. He recognized it as longing, not lust. "I felt it, too. I've wanted you since that night."

Her voice was teasing as she kissed him on the cheek. "You wanted me, and yet your hands were on another man's balls?"

"I was just trying to get his attention." Her scent assailed him and he licked his lips, tasting her. He groaned as her breath in his ear made ignoring her impossible.

She rubbed her hand lightly on his bare stomach as she talked to him. "Then why not take me? We both want it and there's no one here to judge us."

God, he wanted her. Reluctantly, he shook

his head. "Not here, and not now. When we join I have a feeling we'll both be lost in each other. And I want it to be somewhere other than a cave in the forest surrounded by hostiles."

If she'd been standing, she'd have stomped her foot. "Damn it, MacLeod. We could die before that happens."

He grinned at her in the gloom of the cave. "Then I guess we'll just have to stay alive. Besides, your fantasy will probably be better than the real thing. I mean, you being such an experienced woman and all."

She elbowed him hard, and then put her arm over him, snuggling into him. "Damn you. I'm thinking the deed will be much better than the dream. And I've been dreaming since you killed Never-Sleeps in the Osage camp."

Sean came awake slowly, his arm numb and tingly from lying under Ellen. The cave entrance faced the south, and judging by the amount of light casting shadows into the gloom, he figured it was the middle of the afternoon. Ellen groaned softly beside him and sat up. Without speaking, he knew something had awakened both of them. Crawling to the front of the opening, he peered out and saw nothing unusual. Listening intently for a few more moments, he was about to come out when he heard it. The woodchucks were piping their high-pitched bark.

Ellen had come up beside him. "That's why you called them whistle pigs?"

He clamped a hand over her mouth. The sound of someone walking through the leaves left over from last fall drifted to him, and from another direction, the sound of something forcing its way through the light brush populating the hillside.

How many? At least two? More farther out? He only heard the two sounds, but that was no gauge. One thing he did know. If discovered, it would be suicide to be trapped in the cave.

Hoping this was just a rear guard, he decided to chance it. A head-high clump of sumac concealed the front of the cave. Releasing his hold on Ellen, he slowly left the opening.

He immediately saw the two men and stood silently as they seemed to be watching a nest of boulders about fifty yards down the slope and next to the bluff that fell away to the river. They both looked like the river men he'd seen on keelboats and barges wearing boots, homespun pants, and loose shirts. Their beards were unkempt, with long hair shoved up under round caps.

As he watched, one raised his rifle as if to fire a shot toward the boulders below, and then apparently undecided, brought it back down.

Sean slowly pulled his tomahawk from his belt. He'd left his rifle with Ellen, and his bow and quiver were just inside the opening.

"I thought you'd be around here."

A third man! Knowing the man was on the rock directly above him, Sean didn't hesitate. Lunging to the side, he turned and drove the ax into the man's foot.

With a scream, the slaver fell backward, discharging his rifle into the ground at Sean's feet and then disappearing from sight.

The sound of the shot deafened his ears, and the powder smoke burned his eyes, so he didn't hear Ellen scrambling out of the cave. She was holding his rifle, and shoved the long-bow and arrows at him.

She immediately shot at one of the men, catching him in the arm and turning him. By then, Sean had an arrow nocked and shot at the other man. The arrow took him just under the arm, nearly going through him, and he went down coughing blood.

Ellen frantically tried to reload the rifle,

doing a poor job of it, dropping the powder horn to the ground in her haste. She glanced up with panic in her eyes.

The wounded man was trying to bring his rifle to bear on them when Sean shot him. The thrum sound of the bowstring and thump of penetration were almost simultaneous.

The man with the ax wound in his foot crawled away, cussing a blue streak and shouting for help. Farther up the hill, there were answering cries. Grabbing the rifle, shot bag, and powder horn, he shoved the bow into Ellen's hands.

"We gotta go." He pointed downhill. "Get into those rocks. We'll see if there's a way out from there."

She led off, moving quickly between limestone outcroppings and deadfalls as he watched up the hill. There was some movement up where the trail went around the mountain, and it looked like the men weren't quite sure where to come down the slope.

He heard a scream and turned to find Ellen struggling with a man in buckskins.

A big Osage came charging out of the brush from the side. The Indian stopped and fired his musket.

Sean dropped to the ground, white-hot

pain burning across his back, and then leaped up and ran toward Ellen.

The Indian pulled his knife, running at Sean.

When the warrior was close, Sean whipped his longbow across his face, and then stepped in and dispatched him with his hatchet. As the man fell he swiped his knife at Sean, but the dying strength in his arm only left a shallow gash across his chest.

Turning, he saw the other man had Ellen down on her back and her strength waned against the much larger man. Leaping toward them, he hit the man across the back of the head with his ax and he slumped forward on top of Ellen.

He turned, gripping his ax and fighting knife, looking for more men, but the area looked clear of attackers for the moment. He stood taking deep gasps, hands flexing on the handles of his weapons, which were slick with blood. They were partially hidden by the brush and logs on the hillside.

"Dammit, Sean." Ellen's voice was strained and thin, but still full of anger. "Will you get this smelly carcass off me?"

Chuckling, he dragged the man off. She just lay there, breathing hard and looking daggers at him. Her eyes widened when she finally looked closely at him. "Oh, Sean."

He took a moment to look down at himself. The slice across his chest burned like fire and dripped blood. His back felt like he'd been stung by hundreds of hornets. "It's not as bad as it looks. I had to take care of a few things before I could help you."

"Well, it took you long enough."

He continued looking around. His hearing was just coming back, although the ringing was still there. "I figured when you got through playing with that man, you'd let me know."

"Playin' with —"

He reached down and pulled her to her feet. He swatted her bottom and pointed toward the rocks. "Go."

Crouching down, he took a knife, powder horn, and flintlock pistol from the man who'd attacked Ellen. Going farther out, he retrieved the short musket, knife, and leather canteen from the Indian. He thought about the other weapons, but it was too far up the slope to the other dead man. He couldn't chance it now.

He ran back to the boulders. A rockslide had tumbled down the hillside sometime in the past, caught on trees, and made a natural fort about thirty feet across. The ground behind it was packed and held the remains of several campfires.

There was a ghost of a trail coming into the camp, and one going out skirting the bluff overlooking the river. The path was wide open, but if they left, they'd be easy pickings for anyone guarding the trail. In the rocks, it would be hard for anyone to get at them, but just as hard for them to get away.

Ellen came up to him. She looked close to crying and her shoulders slumped in defeat. "There's no way out that isn't exposed. I looked."

He gazed over the ledge at the river below. "I'd guess that's about a fifty foot drop."

She shook her head and finished his thought. "And into knee deep water with rocks on the bottom. We'd break our legs." She stripped off her weapons. With tears in her eyes and a quiver in her voice, she faced Sean. "It's me they want. I'll go."

He smiled at her a moment, shaking his head and marveling at the pure guts of this woman. "The hell you will. You're not going anywhere. Now, get up in those rocks." He handed her the musket.

She started to wipe blood off his chest when he pushed her away. "No time. Now, go."

EIGHTEEN

Sean took stock of their weapons. He had two powder horns that were mostly full, but only about twenty balls left for the long rifle. Ammunition for the large bore musket wasn't a big concern. It would fire anything poked down the barrel, so even rocks would do. There were only ten arrows left in the quiver. After that, it was hand-to-hand with knife and hatchet. And, he had a woman to protect. Not good.

He scrambled up the rocks to join Ellen. She stood on a natural parapet formed by dirt and leaves that had sifted in over the years. Rocks and brush stretched out fifteen feet in either direction and made a natural fort. No one could approach them from the front without scaling about ten feet of smooth boulder. An attack from the sides would expose the enemy for about thirty feet.

Her hand tapping on his shoulder brought

him out of his reverie. "We got company."

He whipped around, searching the forest.

"Not out there."

He turned and looked at her. She pointed to the other side of the ledge they stood on. Lying in a heap of bones and skins was the remains of a man that had been there a long time. Animals and carrion birds had disrupted the open grave.

He stared at the carcass a moment. "Well, I don't think he'll bother us."

"Aren't you just a little curious about how this happened?"

"Not really, but I'll look." He walked around her, letting his hands linger on her as he brushed by. "He was probably a trapper and crawled up here to either hide or defend himself."

Ellen stood where only her eyes were above the protecting rocks, scanning the forest around them. "What makes you think he was a man, and not a woman?"

"Well, I've been around some and I've never seen a woman wearing a coonskin cap."

He suddenly bent forward and pulled something out of the rib cage of the body. "Well, I guess he crawled up here to die. Now we have one more arrow." He scrutinized his find, noting the arrowhead was made of flint. "Although, it looks like mice got the feathers."

"You'd better get over here."

Something in her tone made him go to her immediately. She pointed up the hill to a group of men clustered near a large boulder. As they watched, one man stepped out from the others.

"MacLeod." The slaver's voice carried easily down the hill. "We seem to be at a standoff. You can't get away, and we can't get at you. At least, not yet." The man laughed mockingly. "Of course, we have water and food. Are you and the woman thirsty?"

Sean cursed softly to himself, knowing that was a fair account of their situation. "Ellen, watch to the sides. He'll try to distract us so his men can move in." He stood so the slaver could see him. "It was a bad day when we didn't kill you on the Upper Missouri, Charbonneau."

The man laughed and nodded. "Yes, I suppose you'd see it that way. But, we really can't do much about the past, now can we?"

"No, but we can fix mistakes." The men above spread out.

Charbonneau's laughter was boisterous. The man was putting on a show for his Indian friends. "I'll make you a deal,

MacLeod. If you surrender your weapons and promise to not follow us, I'll let you go free."

"How about you just leave? I like that one better. Better yet, why don't the two of us meet? You choose the weapons."

"Now, that would be foolish. What chance would one man have against the famous Ghostrider? No, I have a prior commitment. We have to meet a flatboat downriver very soon. And we're behind schedule. I don't want you dogging my trail all the way there."

"There's no reason for me to follow you. I have the woman, and her daughter is free."

She hissed at him. "Don't you dare make a deal. They'd kill us in a heartbeat."

He grinned. "Well, me they would. You they'd keep awhile."

"Not if I could find a way to die."

Still watching the men up the hill, he stepped back under cover and pulled her to him. "We need to make sure that doesn't happen, now don't we? Don't hasten death. It comes soon enough to all of us."

One of the Osage couldn't stand the wait any longer and let loose an arrow toward them. Even with the advantage of shooting downhill, the arrow fell short of the rocks.

"What about it, MacLeod? The Osage want blood. The warrior you killed was well liked, a big man in their village." He waited for Sean's reply. When none came, he shook his head. "We'll have the range with the next couple of shots."

The arrow shot from Sean's longbow buried itself in the chest of the Osage that had shot at them. As the Indian writhed on the ground a moment, the rest of the men scrambled for cover.

Sean taunted him again. "How about just you and me, you damned coward? Let's settle this between us."

"You should know better than that. I don't take needless risks. This is how it will be, my men and I will leave. I see no reason to stay and watch you die. And the things they'll do to the woman? Even I don't want to see that. Unfortunately for you, the Osage refuse to leave."

Sean started to take a shot at him, but the man was already turning away. Shifting his aim to one of the closer Indians coming down the hill, he was interrupted by Ellen's warning scream. He turned and saw men coming over the rocks at them from both sides.

Shooting over Ellen's head, he nailed the one closest to her, then turned and put an arrow into the man coming up on his side. Her musket roared behind him, and he wanted to turn, but two Osage were coming up his side of the rocks. Both were huge men, wearing only breechcloths and moccasins, their faces and torsos decorated with bloody handprints. Armed with knives and pipe axes, they stood side by side on the narrow ledge and advanced slowly toward him.

It was quiet behind him, and he desperately wanted to turn and check on Ellen, but he'd have to trust her. She must have grabbed his long rifle, because she shot again. Acrid smoke from the black powder hung in the air, waiting for the breeze to carry it away. She panted for breath as she reloaded the rifle.

Out of arrows, he threw down the bow and pulled his blade and tomahawk. The two Indians were almost on him, and he was tired of fooling around.

A loud whistle sounded from up the hill and it caused the two Osage to hesitate a moment. The one on his left turned his head and looked up the hill, then grunted something to his partner. In the next instant, they attacked. The footing was narrow on the ledge and they were getting in each other's way.

Sean parried a knife thrust from the man on the left while sending his own blade into the warrior's belly. The move pitched the dying man into the other Indian, and as Sean hesitated a moment, a shot sounded behind him. The heavy ball took the remaining Indian in the chest and both attackers collapsed in a heap.

The shot came from right behind him and for the second time that day, he was nearly deaf while surrounded by powder smoke. He turned to see Ellen holding the long rifle, doing a better job of reloading this time, and looking up the slope. He pitched the bodies over the front of the natural parapet and then went to stand beside her. The cut on his chest was bleeding and dripping down his left side.

Several Osage stood in a line up the slope from them, and off to the side he was amazed to see two Osage being chased down by their own people. As he watched, both were dispatched quickly. From the group in front of him, one of the men stepped out.

Ellen came up and leaned into him, offering support, holding a piece of cloth to stop the bleeding.

"Brother Hawk." Sean could hardly believe his eyes, because this wasn't a friend. "Have you come to watch me die?"

Hawk looked at him a moment, and then

looked around at all the bodies littering the slope. "I came to stop the bloodletting so I wouldn't lose any more of my tribe." He gestured around him, shaking his head. "These men who sided with the slavers were renegades, and not true men."

Sean turned that over in his mind a moment. "If that is so, and you want no part of this, did you stop the slavers?"

Hawk just shook his head. "We did not. That is between the whites. It does not concern us."

Ellen shouted, "They have Indian girls."

"True. But not Osage. The young girl you found and returned to us was the only one missing." He beckoned at them. "You may come out now. We will see you to safety and tend to your wounds."

Ellen started to leave, but Sean held her to him. "I think we're fine right where we are." He smiled at the man. "Not that we don't trust you, but as you've said, you don't always have control of your men."

The Indian stared at them a moment, then abruptly nodded. "You are a true man and welcome to trade in our village. Missus Mackey, times change, and my people must change with them or die. For what it's worth, I am sorry for the way you were treated."

Ellen gasped and Sean could tell she was close to tears. "Thank you, Hawk."

As they watched, everyone was gone in moments. A couple of water skins and something wrapped in skin sat on a flat rock. The bodies of the renegade Osage were left where they fell.

Sean turned and leaned against one of the boulders. Ellen immediately tore a long strip from the hem of her shirt and tried to wrap the wound on his chest.

Her soft voice breathed against his chest, and she glanced up at him. "That was unbelievable. I never expected an apology."

He scanned the forest as she worked to stop the bleeding. "I wouldn't put Brother Hawk up on a pedestal just yet."

She tightened the wrap and made him wince. "What do you mean?"

"Keep watching out there where he left the water and food. That was an insult, by the way. He called me a true man, but any man worth his salt can get his own food, and we've a river just behind us for water."

Ellen shook her head. "You've got to get that chip off your shoulder."

She helped him over to a flat place to sit and rest. He was exhausted. "Now I know how that guy felt." He inclined his head toward the pile of bones in the corner. "If you'll keep watch for a few minutes while I catch my breath, I'll take over. After we rest, we'll see about getting out of here."

When he awoke, the day was almost gone and he groaned as he sat up.

"It's about time you woke up. I've about had it and can hardly stay awake." Her voice trailed off as she concentrated on something up the hill. She gave a small gasp. "Well, I'll be damned."

"Osage?" He struggled to his feet.

"Two of them. They were hidden in the brush above the cache of water and food."

She was reaching for the rifle when he stopped her. "Let them go. They were just prospecting. No point in restarting the war."

They climbed down to the lower side where the old campfires were. After gathering enough wood to last the night, he started a fire. Even though it was summer, the night air was chilly along the cold running river. The heat of the fire reflected from the rocks kept them warm during the night. They still had their own water skin, so they huddled together and chewed on dried venison.

He tried to think of what needed to be done. Tomorrow he would down a deer or turkey. Tomorrow. . . .

■ ■ ■ ■

Sean woke with a cold rag bathing his face. When he tried to sit up, Ellen held him down. "Just rest. You've got a fever."

A few minutes later she woke him again. "You've too many wounds and I can't get them clean. I found a path to the river. Come on."

He didn't remember much of the next couple of days. They made it down to the river, because he remembered the pain when she sat him in the shallow water. She washed out all the wounds, restarting the bleeding and cleaning the infection down to raw flesh. He remembered her bandaging him again and taking him to another fire against the bank of the river.

The third day he woke clearheaded. Ellen was asleep next to him and the fire had died down to a slender trail of smoke. She slept with her arms across her knees and had the long rifle and musket next to her. When he stirred, she flinched and came awake.

"Oh, thank God." She reached out and felt his face. The gesture turned into a caress that lingered. "Your fever is gone. I was scared, Sean."

The last few days had drawn on her

strength. She looked worn out. He sat up and looked down at himself. "Where'd you get the bandages?"

She chuckled. "Well, let's just say I'm not wearing underwear anymore."

His imagination ran wild a moment and he gave her a small smile. "Sorry I missed the show. Thank you for what you've done."

When he tried to get up, she held him back. "Eat first, then we'll see how well you can walk. I took a chance and shot a deer when they came down for water this morning." She grimaced, holding her shoulder. "I tried to use your bow. How do you pull that thing?"

He was amazed and wondered where she found an arrow. Then he realized where and hated she'd had to do that. "The sound of you shooting didn't even wake me?"

She just shook her head. "You were not yourself."

Minutes later, she'd suspended meat over the fire. As it cooked he spoke to her, wondering if she could hear his stomach growl. "We won't have to cook it long. I could eat it raw." Looking around, he sighed. "I could get used to this."

"Get used to what? Being cut up and shot?"

He reached out and pulled her to him,

careful of his side. "I could get used to you taking care of me."

"Well, don't get used to it. You're not a child and neither am I. Don't think you're just going to grab me up and throw me into your cabin or wikiup."

"I don't have a cabin yet and right here would be just fine. We've a nice fire, warm blankets, and cool water if we get too sweaty." His voice was purposefully mild as he smiled at her. For some reason, storm clouds gathered on her brow. "No, huh? Well, you've changed your tune since the cave the other night."

Ellen pulled away from him. "I lost my head for a time. I'm not like that. Most men think since I have a half-breed child that I'm easy or a whore. I don't just spread my legs for anyone, and for your information I haven't done that since I had Beth."

He quickly reached out and grabbed the back of her head. Gripping her by the hair, he brought her to him and kissed her. Not giving her time to respond, he abruptly pushed her away. "You have a child, not a half-breed. I'd never think of you that way, or Beth. Any man who says that will answer to me."

Tears in her eyes, she started to answer when he interrupted her. "Let's eat and get out of here. You need to see your daughter and I've got better places to be."

NINETEEN

Sean couldn't walk very far without resting, and Ellen was tired, although she wouldn't admit it. It took them two days before they walked into the compound at Jones Mill. There were few people about and the first thing he heard was a shrill whinny from Thunder. He walked to the horse as Ellen continued on to her cabin in silence. His troubled gaze followed her. She was excited to see her daughter, but had hardly spoken a word to him since the river. Any attempt he'd made to talk with her was shut down. Turning once, it looked like she wanted to say something to him, but then she trudged on toward her cabin.

His thoughts were interrupted by Rob Shay all but busting the door of the building off its hinges as he rushed outside.

"Sean MacLeod. We thought you and Ellen had died."

"It was a close thing, Shay."

Sean was dragged into the bar with hand shaking and backslapping, each bringing a grimace from him. "Shay, why don't you set me up with some mystery meat and rum, and tell me what's been going on."

He sat in the same place at the bar that he'd been just a few days before. Somehow, it felt like a long time. So much had happened and too many had died.

When Shay brought the food and drink, he settled on a bar stool next to him. Jones brought him a new shirt. Both men settled and watched him eat. He could tell Shay was busting to talk, but waited until he at least had some food in his belly.

Having been silent for the half hour it took for that to happen, Shay told him what had happened. "A runner came in with a message from Red Eagle just yesterday. The Cherokee and their friends caught the slavers where you said they'd be. From what I understood, it wasn't much of a fight, but sure left a lot of bodies floating in the river."

Sean wearily shook his head. "Nobody will miss them. What about Santee?"

"Well, seems he never made it. Once he accidentally got away, he turned and headed west as if he was trying to get away. Those Cherokee following him wanted to go south, so they just took his hair so they could catch up for the big fight. They said he begged like a baby."

Sean stopped chewing and looked at Shay, trying to stay awake. "What about Charbonneau? Did they kill him?"

"Nope. They said he wasn't with the slavers. Maybe he was cagey enough to suspect an ambush and took off for better pastures."

He told Shay how the Osage had come and saved them, and then about the trap they'd set for them later.

Shay shrugged and took another drink of rum. "No accounting for that. They're a strange people. Pray for ya one minute, then kill ya the next."

Sean pushed his plate away. "I've just got to have some rest. Do me a favor and make sure Ellen gets settled in. After me leaning on her for two days, she's exhausted and about to drop. She'll need clothes and like me she's probably too tired to cook. I don't think she could have taken much more out there. I've got some loose ends to take care of, and then I'll be pullin' out."

"Pullin' out? I thought, maybe . . . ?"

"She's got different ideas on that." He looked at Shay, kind of dreading the answer. "I assume Buffalo Shield is still around."

"Aye. That he is. He's waiting for you."

Thinking about their vow of blood, he just grunted. Right now, he didn't feel much like he could take on a baby Blackfoot, much less a full-grown one. "Well, he can just wait."

Shay cleared his throat a couple of times, looking everywhere but at him.

"Spit it out, Shay."

"Well," he hesitated a moment. "That Blackfoot ain't that bad a guy, once you get to know him. He's been hangin' around with Ellen's daughter ever since he brought her in and makin' some good suggestions. I think the girl has turned him around a bit."

"Suggestions? What kind of suggestions?"

Shay looked up defiantly. "Well, if you weren't so tired you might have noticed we're kinda short of soldiers since Captain Frane got himself ambushed and committed suicide."

"Suicide?"

"A couple of soldiers got away. They'd been hanging back, for some reason. They said the good captain was so afraid of being captured he shot himself at the first war whoop. Maybe it was an accident. Dunno."

He shook his head. "I'm not believing that. What about Buffalo Shield?"

Shay continued his story. "Old Buffalo Shield suggested we start clearing brush from the back sides of the buildings so no one could sneak up on us. He made some other suggestions to help. According to him, a herd of ten-year-old Osage girls could run right over us and we wouldn't be able to stop it."

He held up his hand. "Shay, for the life of me I'm too tired to try and keep up with you. Save it for later."

They took him to a room above the store and he dropped fully-clothed to the cot on top of the blankets. His last thoughts were of a herd of girls that looked like Beth running rampant over the landscape. He was asleep in seconds.

Sean awoke the next morning with a pounding headache and nearly cried out from pain when he rolled out of bed and wound up on his hands and knees. Stiff and sore, he finally made it to his feet and moved around like an old man with palsy. A new set of clothes were laid out on the foot of the bed. He bathed from a bucket of water sitting on the side table, and then dressed. His wounds still felt tight, and the healing scar across his chest impeded the use of his left arm. Looking in a polished metal mirror, he decided he could use a haircut and vowed to find a soaking bath soon. The river water was just too damned cold.

When he finally walked into the bar, Shay sat at a table reading a bundle of papers.

"Glad to see you're still alive." He waved the papers at Sean. "I guess we'll be a state next year. Don't really know why. Seems like them politicians stir up more trouble than they fix."

"Has Ellen been in?"

"Nope. Just her daughter. If you're interested, she lives on the north side of the compound, just beyond the trees."

After eating breakfast, he stood on the porch of the trading post. It was a cool morning with a slight breeze coming off the river. He took a deep breath and immediately regretted it and started coughing, holding his hand to his side. Across the way, a couple of soldiers lounged at the front of their depot. Two saddle horses were tied to the rail, standing hipshot and sleepy. He wondered how long it would be before they got a new captain commander.

To his right was the stable, his own horse, and an easy way out. A smart man would take it. If he went left, he'd run into Ellen's house. Butterflies invaded his belly every time he thought of that. Finally, he stepped off the porch.

"Ah, my friend MacLeod."

He whirled to see Charbonneau leading his horse from around the building. His hands went to his waist, only to come up empty. All his weapons were in the room upstairs. Slowly, seemingly in degrees, he relaxed. Maybe he could get close enough. . . .

Charbonneau paused to pull a long saber from the scabbard on his saddle and slashed it through the air a couple of times, practicing. "You have caused me much trouble and money. I could easily shoot you, but this way is more appropriate, don't you think? It's time to end this."

"I'm unarmed." There was movement over the man's shoulder.

Charbonneau laughed. "But of course. So much the better. Did you lose your famous fighting knife? The Spanish blade I've heard so much about?"

"You're a coward." He backed into the compound to give himself more room to maneuver. Old Angus MacLeod had taught him how to deal with this situation. But if Charbonneau was any good with that saber it wouldn't matter. And he was tired.

The man advanced toward him. "Say goodbye, MacLeod. I'm going to enjoy this."

An arrow punched completely through Charbonneau's chest from the back, narrowly missing Sean, speckling his face and new shirt with blood. He looked up beyond Charbonneau, and saw Buffalo Shield holding his English longbow. Beth Mackey was beside him.

Charbonneau fell to the ground. He tried once to draw up his knee and rise, and then went limp and settled into the dust.

Sean shook his head in wonder, thankful he was alive. "That man always was a talker. I guess he finally talked himself to death. Thanks, Buffalo Shield. That was a nice shot. How are you Beth?"

"I'm good. Are you hurt? It looks like you're bleeding again."

"Not this time. It's not my blood."

People streamed out of the buildings to look at the body.

Buffalo Shield walked up to Sean and pushed on his chest. Sean flinched away, guarding his side. "You are in no shape to fight, so I tried out your bow."

Sean held his elbow tight into his side, trying to will the pain to go away. "You may have it, as my gift to you."

The old Indian shrugged. "I couldn't have you getting hurt more. I'm still waiting. It is a strange thing that I have to protect you just so we can have a remembered battle. There must be blood between us."

Beth wedged between the two men, looking up at Buffalo Shield. "Grandfather. Remember what we talked about."

The two men stared at each other for a moment, and then Buffalo Shield dropped his gaze to the girl.

"It cannot always be as you wish, Granddaughter. Some things have to be done." He looked back at Sean with the beginning of a smile. "It seems I have a family again."

Beth looked at both of them a moment, and then reached over and pulled a knife from Buffalo Shield's waistband. She took his palm and made a small cut on the pad below the thumb, and then did the same with Sean. "Put your hands together."

Again, they warily watched each other until finally Buffalo Shield made the first move and shook Sean's hand.

Beth held their hands together. "Now, there has been blood. Your vow has been kept. My grandfather can send word back to the Blackfoot nation that there has been blood and the feud is over. It is at an end."

Sean looked at Buffalo Shield and shook his head. "When did she get so bossy?"

The old medicine man snorted and shook his head. "I did not know she was my granddaughter until she told me she had adopted me. Sometimes there are forces around us that we cannot control."

"How old are you?" The girl ignored Sean's question.

Beth finally released their hands, and looked at Sean. "You men are strange, and sometimes stupid." She pointed toward the trees. "Our cabin is over there. I believe my mother is home."

He was surrounded by a half circle of friends. Rob Shay and Jones blocked the way to the stables. The few remaining soldiers stood around grinning at him. There was only one way to go. A few steps that seemed to take forever took him to Ellen's door. Under the cool shade of the trees, his first step onto the porch moved a loose board and he paused for a moment, looking around. The place needed a lot of work, but the big job was inside.

He walked in without knocking and found her sitting at a table made from rough slabs of oak and holding a pewter mug. Startled, she jumped up, holding her hand to her chest as her chair scooted backwards and fell over onto the plank floor with a thud. She was dressed in a blue homespun dress and her hair was done up with a matching blue ribbon. They stared at each other for a long moment, her eyes welling with unshed tears.

Finally, he held up his cut hand. "I'm hurt. Will you take care of me?"

It was hard to keep from getting blood on that dress.

ABOUT THE AUTHOR

Darrel Sparkman resides in Southwest Missouri with his wife. Their three children and eleven grandchildren live nearby. His hobbies include gardening, golfing, and writing. In the past, Darrel served four years in the United States Navy, including seven months in Viet Nam as a combat search & rescue helicopter crewman. He also served nineteen years as a volunteer Emergency Medical Technician, worked as a professional photographer, computer repair tech, and was owner and operator of a greenhouse and flower shop. Darrel is currently retired and self-employed. He finally has that job that wakes you up every day with a smile.

The employees of Thorndike Press hope you have enjoyed this Large Print book. All our Thorndike, Wheeler, and Kennebec Large Print titles are designed for easy reading, and all our books are made to last. Other Thorndike Press Large Print books are available at your library, through selected bookstores, or directly from us.

For information about titles, please call:
(800) 223-1244

or visit our website at:
gale.com/thorndike

To share your comments, please write:
Publisher
Thorndike Press
10 Water St., Suite 310
Waterville, ME 04901